pseud Calhoun

The Stenographer, His Life, Trials, and Difficulties

Together with many of the perplexing circumstances which often confront him

pseud Calhoun

The Stenographer, His Life, Trials, and Difficulties
Together with many of the perplexing circumstances which often confront him

ISBN/EAN: 9783337149352

Printed in Europe, USA, Canada, Australia, Japan

Cover: Foto ©Andreas Hilbeck / pixelio.de

More available books at **www.hansebooks.com**

THE
STENOGRAPHER,

His Life, Trials and Difficulties,

Together with Many of the Perplexing
Circumstances which often
confront him.

BY

"CALHOUN,"
Who has been through the "Mill."

Also contains many valuable instructions to Stenographers which will enable
them to avoid many difficulties and errors,
if carefully perused. We cannot live our life
over again, hence let us profit by the experience of others.

"In the lexicon of youth which fate,
reserves for a bright manhood, there is
no such word as—fail."

PUBLISHED BY
THE STENOGRAPHIC BOOK COMPANY,
St. Louis, Mo.
1894.

PREFACE.

It is not with a view of astonishing the literary world that this volume is published, but that something might be done to encourage those of my profession. Works of all kinds and classes have been introduced, nearly every profession has some work of its kind, but thus far the poor stenographer has been left in the cold. And why thus? We have feet that walk and hearts that beat and that have feeling as well as any other class of individuals.

This work is not intended only to please the mind of the one who may casually glance over its pages, but those who may think their future presents a gloomy appearance cannot help but feel encouraged after reading the contents found in this book. We as a class of willing workers are rapidly reaching the point where the world cannot do without us. The prospects before the stenographer were never brighter, and to those who are but starting in the profession, weary not in the undertaking. There is yet a wonderful ladder before you, many who now hold positions of trust and honor started as a stenographer. To the one yet in school let me say, labor diligently, work earnestly, and do not become discouraged because the top of the ladder is not reached in a day. When you once become proficient in your profession there will always be avenues thrown open before you by which you can earn a good salary.

If in this work, the effort will be the means of assisting those of the profession in any way, the time will be considered as well invested. There is no more noble calling for a young lady than to become a good stenographer, it enables her to become independent, self supporting and worthy of the admiration of all.

In this work it has been deemed advisable to be plain spoken, and with the exception of names being substituted, there is no novel about it, it is a reality, the circumstances actually transpiring. Perhaps in some places the brush may have rubbed a little roughly, but some of the incidents have been an awful reality to the writer. Stenographic friends, push forward, seek to advance your employers' interests, and they will not fail to appreciate the effort and reciprocate.

CONTENTS.

CHAPTER I.

"Say, Father, I've got a sort of a sneaking idea I would like to learn shorthand and be a stenographer; if you'll give me a little wad of currency to use attending school, I will try and make my own way in the world after that."

"That's just like some of your high-toned ideas. Why can't you go to school and study some of the ordinary branches like the other boys did? You are always on the wrong road and wanting something you can't have. We never more than get one of your wants satisfied until you are originating another."

"Yes; but I have been reading those papers the fellows sent me from the school up there in Iowa where it says in three months I could fix myself up for a good stenographer, and in six months be a court reporter, and of course nothing short of a court reporter would stop me. Just think of only attending school from four to six months and then get a salary of from,—Oh, I don't know how much, but after three months I could easily get from $60.00 to $75.00 per month without a bit of trouble, and I have made up my mind I want to go. If you will not furnish me the necessary wherewith, I will borrow it and go anyhow."

"That all sounds well enough to talk about, but I guess you will find people are not so hungry for reporters and stenographers as you think they are."

"I read it myself in the circular which the school man sent me, and of course he would not misrepresent it in the least. It says 'good men always in demand,' so you see there would be no trouble whatever for me."

"Oh, well, if you are so determined, we will see about it later on, but I am satisfied you are making the mistake of your life."

Such was the conversation which took place between a long, lank-looking country boy who answered to the name of "Jack," and a somewhat aged man, who was his sire. Jack was made up something after the fashion of the average Northern Missouri farm boy of the age; his wardrobe consisted of about as meagre a make-up as the law allowed—straw hat, hickory shirt, trousers and some large looking articles which he called shoes. The little articles which most men wear, commonly called socks, were looked upon by him as a sort of luxury and were only to be worn in cold weather. The trousers, whether from an idea of economy or because of shrinkage, we are not at present in a position to state, but sufficeth to say, they lacked about two inches of making connection with the top of his shoes. They were kept suspended and held in their proper locality by the means of a string business across the shoulder, better known among the boys as a "gallus." It depended largely upon circumstances whether or not two of these "galluses" were used or only one, as one would answer the purpose fairly well, and everything went to show that he had a great dislike for superfluous wearing apparel.

The old gentleman was more respectable looking, being dressed in a modern farmer style, and while he was quite a congenial old fellow the fact was very evident that he did not in the least approve of Jack's going away to school to squander money and time in attempting to learn something that he would never be able to realize anything from. Times were hard and money market close, especially in that locality, besides the money necessary to equip the young enthusiast would buy ever so many good calves then for sale in the country; this all had a bearing at this critical moment. However, Jack was persistent, and as there was an intervening space of two or three months before the time arrived for him to take up his departure for the much coveted locality, the matter rested where it was for the present, sort o' between heaven and earth as it were, or at least so it appeared to Jack.

We deem it proper here to give a brief account of what farm life was at that time in that part of Missouri, in order that the reader more fully appreciate the circumstances which surrounded and the duties involved upon us, at the time we first determined to give vent to the growing ambition and leave the farm.

The true American is born with that spirit of unrest in him that is never satisfied until death has ushered in the change that puts the finishing touch on our earthly career. I was no exception to this rule, hence the excitement that enters into life on the farm failed entirely to satisfy or gratify my ambitious desires. Everything was passing along with such a dull expected sameness, the hills were just where they had been for years, the trees that I had watched and played under in childhood, still continued to put forth their leaves in springtime, and with exactly the same regularity become barren in winter. The creek that ran near the house was precisely the same it had been ever since I could remember, and in short I was disgusted with everything; besides, it seemed my work was never done; all work and no play. I thought I was the most unfortunate creature on the face of the globe, and that everyone else was sailing along on flowery beds of ease. How little did I realize what the then undeveloped future held in store for me, and how many times have I looked back since and thought how those might have been the most pleasant days of my life. Father, mother, brothers and sisters, all at home in one happy family. Often and often have I longed but for one more such gathering, but it is impossible. How true the maxim, We never know when we have a good thing until it is too late. I little dreamed what city life was, as I had never been in a town of any size since I was a mere child, and of course was comparatively ignorant concerning its mysteries, but the brush of meditation had been busy for many months painting upon the panorama of my imagination the wonders and excitement that such a life held in store for me. I had cherished the hope so long and so fondly that it had reached the point where nothing short of that seemed to hold any inducement or have any satisfaction for me whatever. The fire of life had been ignited; the brush continued to paint, and every stroke assisted but to fan the smouldering fire of ambition into flames. So it is with the one shut up in the city; if they could but have more of their time to invest upon the farm or rural retreats, as they are pleased to term it, how grand it would be. How much more life would be worth living if we could but be satisfied with our lot; how much more we could get out of life, and how it would tend to raise the standard of human existence.

It is hardly necessary for me to go away back and tell you who my grandmothers and grandfathers were on both sides for a number of decades and generations, and for two reasons I refrain from doing so, first, because it would not particularly interest any, and second, I am not in a position just now to do so, as most of them had passed over the river before I came upon the stage of action.   I knew but a grandfather and a grandmother, personally.

We first saw the sun rise in the state of Illinois, in the central part, Livingston county, and as I am still in a state of celibacy I withhold announc- ing the date of my first appearance upon the arena, but to say that it has been many moons, is placing it mildly.   My parents moved from that state to the northern part of Missouri when I had but passed the second mile post of my existence, con- sequently I know very little of my historical career or maneuvers in that part of the vineyard.   The song I learned to sing when young expresses, to a great degree, the surroundings, which was some- thing like the following:

"Amid broad fields of wheat and corn,
The lovely home where I was born."

The northern part of Missouri in the seventies was hardly in a perfect state of civilization.   'Tis true the Indian had been driven farther west, and the most ferocious wild animals slaughtered or had their minds impressed with the fact that it was no place for them and migrated of their own accord. That class of people who are never exactly con- tented unless they are on the frontier and leading a pioneer life, made up a greater portion of the population.   While they might have been ever so friendly and sociable, they were not satisfied with the thought of the country being so thickly set- tled as to render hunting of no avail, and of course soon pushed farther west.

I remember very distinctly of having the principles of the English alphabet inculcated into my
cranium while sitting on a bench made of a
slab, with holes bored through it and pegs put in
to hold it up. 'Twas a sort of "Abraham Lin-
coln" or "Andrew Jackson" school house. In
fact this is the way many great men got their
start, the only trouble with this one being, it was
not made of logs, or who knows what the result
might have been with me? It was really a nice,
but dirty old place, the birds using the upper part
for nesting and caring for their young, vermin
using the lower realms for various purposes; we
occupied the center. Despite all this the location was beautiful, the elegant natural grove behind the house and the fine lawn in front of it
were really inviting; but to be frank about the
matter, the building itself and those hard old slab
benches do not occupy a very warm place in my
heart. This, however, only lasted about a year
and a half of my school days, as the district became so far advanced in civilization they erected
a new school house, and got so rashly extravagant
as to paint it white. Neighboring districts looked
upon this as an outlandish outlay of means, for to
add to all this terrible display of wealth, they had
"boughten" seats on the inside. How proud we
were, and how much easier it was for the kids to
sit still when they could have something to place
their poor, lean backs against, and not have more
than two others in the seat with them. With four

or five boys all sitting on one slab bench, it is next to impossible to keep them all from sliding up in a bunch, and then what follows is too well known to need relating. The erection of the schoolhouse in our district appeared to eventually dawn upon the obtuse minds of the adjoining districts that perhaps it was a tolerably good thing, so some of the rest tried, and soon the old pioneer school houses began to lose their grip and were replaced by new ones.

I always was a sort of a meek kid and too big a coward to fight, hence I escaped many a black eye which a majority of school boys had the pleasure of wearing. While small I was usually of fair deportment, and the teacher seldom had occasion to administer corporal punishment. Such things as getting ears twisted considerably out of their ordinary posture, nose pulled, or fingers thumped with a ruler were only daily occurrences, and of course I had my share of them. I remember quite clearly of having committed some little misdemeanor one day and as a punishment for the same I was compelled to go over and sit beside one of the gentler sex. Then, it was to me the most severe and cruel punishment and looked upon as dreadful treatment, but I have often thought since, what a fool I was. The lessons of life are never completely learned until it is too late to take advantage of opportunities, and when we have a good thing we never have sense enough to appreciate it.

Most all boys, I believe, think school days are the most horrible of their lives; that is, in their earlier school days. It seems, fish will never bite better than during the very time they are at school; they never have a greater desire to help mother than at about nine in the morning, and in short it seems like a prison, that dull, dirty school room. I was no exception to the rule in this line and could not help thinking they were mistreating me very much by compelling me to go to school, for of course I went with no other thought than of it being a case of absolute necessity. Most parents like to have the kids say they "like to go," "enjoy school," etc., and my oldest sister was very anxious that I should be in this mood. One morning on being questioned on this point by a gentleman, "Do you like to go to school?" I frankly answered, "No, sir." 'Tis needless to say I got a lecturing, and promised I would answer affirmatively henceforth, and so I did, although I often knew it was prevaricating.

The inducements to get a child to attend school were then very poor as compared with the more modern system. Then we were supposed to grasp and dig out education, or a start at least from the "three R" system. Everything was fed cold and not always in broken doses either. There was one rule, "get your lesson or take a licking," which was usually more or less respected.

I continued in this way until I began to verge into my teens without anything very startling happening to mar the quietness thereof.

CHAPTER II.

As year after year wore away, some of the childish ideas began to relax their hold upon me and I commenced to look at school as at least a few grades above penitentiary life, and by stretching the word truth to its extreme limit, I might say that ere I was fifteen I looked upon attending the place where education was dished up, with a slight degree of pleasure. This had partially been brought about by a number of circumstances which have a tendency to mould the ideas of a boy who is not naturally over-ambitious to engage in the labor presenting itself on a farm. By this time I had learned to follow the plow with becoming dignity, wield the hoe in the weed patch, extract the lacteal fluid from the bovine groupe, and various other little duties wherein I could make myself useful as well as ornamental. It might be well to here add that, like most other boys, about the only things I was naturally adapted to, was fishing and eating, or chasing the grey squirrel through the woods, or at other times follow a rabbit track, which was a day or two old, for a few miles. Of course I had all the ailments and dis-

eases common to growing kids; possibly I skipped
one or two of the category, but among the ones
yet firmly impressed upon my memory I might
enumerate chicken-pox, mumps, measles and itch.
The latter named disease was of the seven-year
variety; however, by luxurious and persistent use
of sulphur we succeeded in curtailing its career to
a certain extent. I believe of the list, this one
has left the most lasting impression.

I usually attended the tabernacle of learning
about nine months in the year until sixteen; after
that, would attend about four, forgetting during
the eight what I learned during the four, hence
just about retained my intellectual equilibrium for
a few years. It was the custom in those days to
have the kids give a sort of a young exhibition of
their oratorical ability on Friday afternoons, which
consisted of a little poetry, partially committed to
memory, select reading, or a composition. While
I did not take kindly to any of these, I usually, as
a matter of policy, performed enough to stay the
wrath of those in power and held legal authority
to wield the rod of correction. To give you a
slight idea of the effort I sometimes put forth, I
insert one of my compositions on Christopher
Columbus:

"CHRISTOPHER COLUMBUS.

"It is said that Columbus discovered America,
but now the question arises how did he discover
it. He, according to history, had a powerful hard
time to get started across the deep. Well, ac-

cording to history he went whineing around trying to get some of his friends to throw in 5 cents
to help him get started, but just about the time he
had commenced to get his influence over the people there was some fellows took the advantage of
poor old Chris, and one day got in a boat
and went out 15 or 20 miles, as they thought, and
looked as far as they could see, but they could
not see land, so they went back and said that
Columbus' plan was a fraud.

"This completely bumswizzled Columbus, so he
went home discouraged, but he was a man that
would not yield to discouragement.

"So in a few centuries he again tried his luck
and succeeded.   Chris. Columbus started from
England to discover America; he was the happy
owner of a small row boat and two hoop-poles for
propellers.   He took with him a loaf of bread, a
clam basket and an old ham bone, also his brother
Nicodemus.   His brother had a hat that meas-
ured five miles around the brim.   He took with
him for society, a pig, a cat and a rat, and for
fear they would quarrel he placed the rat in the
sugar bowl, the cat in the salt box and the pig in
the cabin.   Columbus had an immense watch;
the hour hand was five feet long.

"One day the pig took a walk on the deck and
got dizzy and fell overboard and was drowned.
He was 2 years, 3 months, 4 weeks, 5 days, 6 hours,
30 min,. 50 sec. old at the time of his death.
Soon after this Columbus discovered "Cat Is-

land," so named on account of the tremendous number of cats that peopled the island, this is an island that is in America. Poor old Chris is dead now and gone away."

Human nature has peculiar freaks which sometimes we are at a loss to explain, but to me one of the deepest, darkest mysteries, and one which I am at a loss to interpret is, why even a school boy will acquire such a strong affinity for a sister other than his own. A fifteen year old boy will work himself half to death tugging at a sled, when there is a pretty little girl perched thereon, provided she is not his sister, while he could not think of exerting such an effort on her behalf under any circumstances. Most boys at this age, especially while attending school, gradually become to think a great deal more of some certain girl of about their own age than any others, and this thought harbored and cherished month after month, he finally imagines, perhaps before he has reached eighteen, that he is really in the hands of cupid, and unless he shall some day have her undivided attention, life will be but an empty shell. I now look back over that time and say "What fools we mortals be." Here again I was no exception to the rule, and encountered fully my proportion of the ups and downs brought about by such action.

When about sixteen an incident in my life occurred which came near causing me to join the silent majority. The reptiles known as a "rattlesnake" were quite numerous in that vicinity, and their bite was usually looked upon as fatal. I was in the field one day in the summer, and as the weather was very pleasant and warm I removed the large boots from my feet and began meandering around barefooted. I had only kept this up a short while when I stepped directly on a rattlesnake, and was of course bitten. It had only been a short time before that a little girl, one of the neighbor's, had been similarly afflicted and had resulted in death. The first thought that flew across my mind was to slay the intruder, which act was accomplished with due deliberation; then came the thought which has for ages perplexed nations, "Where will I go if I die?

. I did not then look upon death in the same light that I now do, or perhaps it would have appeared less terrible; then, it presented an awful picture to my excited imagination. About all I could get into my cranium was, Jack laid out, funeral procession, hole in the ground about five feet long and then! Then, all was blank. I had never studied the mysteries of the future, other than what I had occasionally heard from mother or the Sunday school teacher. Their spiritual admonition had been looked upon very lightly, but now the mean things I had done began to flood my troubled brain to a desperate degree. 'Tis easy enough to talk about dying, while in good health, but when it comes to the point where we realize it is on the verge of reality, or when

one thinks his time has come to cross the gulf, the
matter appears altogether different.   I was about
three miles from home when the accident occurred,
and, as was the custom, the first thing to do in
cases of that kind was to dope the invalid with
whiskey.   My brother came to my rescue and we
secured some of the fiery drug from a neighboring house.   The first "swig" I took came near
cheating the snake bite out of its glory, as it was so
strong it came near strangling me, for in the excited state I was then in, I took much more than
should have been given to one of my age.   After
a brief struggle I commenced to breathe with a
little less effort.   About this time another old time
remedy was applied—that of burning the wound
with a view of the fire drawing the poison out.   I
afterwards discovered that such a remedy was
perhaps all right in theory, but it fell far short in
actual practice, for the burning hurt so I could
not endure it, and furthermore would not.   The
fire burning at my foot, the whiskey internally getting in its work, and my agitated brain, all worked
in unison to make life exceedingly lively for a season.   By the time we reached home the afflicted
member had swollen to considerably above its
normal state.   The excitement around home which
would naturally follow, took place.   I was chucked
into bed, the whiskey supply replenished by one
of the boys going seven miles to the nearest village; in the meantime I was being doped with
what the neighbors had, my foot soaked in various

poison antidotes, and everything being done that possibly could be to thwart the purpose of Mr. Snake. About 6 p. m., (the wound having been inflicted·about 2 p. m.) the whiskey began to affect me quite severely, and before seven, I was really drunk. I shall never forget the feeling, how very queer it was; have never been in such a condition since, either from snake or liquor trouble, but that once gave me an experience never to be forgotten. It happened the family were all out of the room at this time, and despite the swollen foot, I got out of bed and ran out into the yard and acted as one just escaping from a lunatic asylum. Whether the whiskey, fire or the other antidotes applied did the work, I am unable to say, but before midnight the pain had become very materially lessened and the danger was over. After a few days remaining in bed, I was again on my feet, but my foot being left in a very bad condition it was deemed wise to not allow me to travel around very much, hence I was again allowed to attend school.

About this time there was a family from one of the eastern states came west and located in our immediate vicinity, about two miles from where we lived. The country west of us was rough and cover-with light timber, east of us was prairie. As circumstances so happened, this family lived west. While the family of itself was nothing extraordinary, there was one member of it, being of the female persuasion, that was to my then inexperienced mind considerably out of the common line.

Imported articles are presumably the best always, and perhaps this was one reason why I looked upon this new comer with so much favor. To do her justice, however, she was a little ahead of the average girl that then inhabited that strip of the woods, and it is nothing more than right that I here admit I was always quite easily influenced by the gentler sex, and am not in a position to say that it is entirely outgrown yet, but materially improved in this respect. Jennie McGinnis was a girl with such a quick, sharp eye, honest countenance and industrious, that one could not help admiring her; and then, I am now convinced she was a little coquettish. It cannot be denied that I thought she was "pretty fine," and she had no hesitancy in showing by her actions that my attentions were cordially received and that she was a firm believer in reciprocity. Talk about backwoods courtship! * * * The following year held much in store for me. I was such a frequenter at the McGinnis house that even the dog became to treat me as one of the family, and of course, as boys always are, I was as much in love with the whole family as with the girl, but naturally preferred her solitary association to that of the entire generation. A fellow has got to have an abundance of tenacity to successfully wait upon a young lady in such localities. The entire family, including the dog, congregate in the select room during the evening, and regardless of who was present or previous conditions of servitude the old gentleman, the old lady and a regular generation of children would take up their post and stand by it manfully. Of course I had my place. I'd play with the kids, talk to the old man about crops, politics, religion and measles, and then turn and talk to the old lady about the neighbors awhile, and occasionally wink at the girl. After keeping this up for a few hours the kids would begin to wilt like a summer Four O'clock in the sun, and as kid after kid would go down and be grappled in the arms of morpheus, the elder children would drag them off to bed. Occasionally the dragee would be aroused by the rough treatment he received, and the conversation that would immediately follow, at times had a tendency to embarrass a fellow a little, especially when considering the surroundings; this, however, one soon became accustomed to, and when the occasion demanded could help drag the young intruders out with pretty good grace, for by so doing it hastened the time when I should have the undivided attention of Miss Jennie. After the little offsprings had all been dumped into their sleeping apartments and the dust which had been agitated by the recent struggle, had cleared away, the old man would start in afresh, tell a string or two of fish stories, each of which I knew I had to pay strict attention to in order to hold my job. Of course I would always laugh heartily, even though the tales be as dry as chips. Every time the old man would give a good big yawn I would take fresh

courage, for I knew the time was fast approaching
when he would succumb to the inevitable attack
of morpheus. When the opportunity presented
itself, I would try and get in a few words to the
effect that aged people required more sleep than
middle aged or young people, but despite all my
efforts the antique gentleman would remain faith-·
fully at his post until it would seem I must give up
in despair. His better half would, if she happened to notice my uneasy posture and restless
disposition, broach the subject of retiring. This
would sometimes prove effective, at other times
cause but a look at the clock, stretch of the body
and enable him to start off on another line of fish
stories, or tales of the wonderful land of "back
where I come from." 'Tis needless to say that I
invariably agreed with him on all points, regardless of whether on neighbors, cattle, church or
state, although at the time I might know he was
prevaricating, perhaps unintentionally. What a
dickens of a time he did have with those oxen
when he was a boy! I have never forgotten all
those tales, not by consiberable, and as they so
cruelly punished me I would not think of administering them to others with any thought of enter-
tainment or knowledge.

I have always entertained a friendly feeling for
the mother, partially for the kindness shown me
during my visits there, and the very material
assistance furnished me in later years, which may
be explained further on.

CHAPTER III

DIFFICULTIES ATTENDING COUNTRY LIFE.

As all things come to those who wait, so it would be on occasions of this nature, for finally sleep would approach them with such terrible velocity they must answer its calls. The heavy boots withdrawn and the nether garments of the foot, commonly called hosiery (which we might add were non-odorless) dislodged and placed in the proper receptacle, much to my glory they would take their departure, not however without cautiously warning Jennie against remaining up late.

I am not an advocate of late hour keeping, but under such circumstances I believe if ever a fellow is warranted in holding forth until the short hours of the morning, under such he certainly would be, and so thought I then. We were both bashful, and the dreadful quietness which seized the room when the chatter which had been permeating the atmosphere with such startling rapidity for hours had become a thing of the past, it almost caused one to think of a funeral, and all those beautiful thoughts that had been cherished for two or three days to tell her when the opportunity pre-

sented itself, now vanished. There is a stillness
which has a terror; such this would be occasionally; however, we were both aware of the fact that
the more quietness that prevailed just now, the
earlier the time would be marked when the head
of the ranch would be dreaming of those oxen and
potatoes. Of course we could so arrange matters
that we would not be compelled to talk very loud
that the other might hear * * * and would get
along fairly well for a few hours, but you may imagine about what time the clock would register ere
this. Two long miles through the timber and a
very rough road before I could reach home, perhaps the weather cold, or dark and rainy; if the
latter, to say the least, it was a terrible trip, for
in places the road was almost impassable, and then
there is always a dreadful fear that haunts boys
when called upon to pass through heavy timber on
occasions like this. The trees each apparently
harbor some formidable creature with eyes glaring
at you, or claws outstretched, ready to light upon
your quivering frame as you pass. More than
once in making this trip, which I did very frequently, has my hair been caused to seemingly
turn to bristles, and my heart beat like a drum-
stick, and on such occasions I would solemnly decide in my own mind that never would I remain
so late again, but on the next occasion the very
same hour would perhaps call my departure from
the cottage where the flower of my existence held
forth.

Charity is like truth, it is mighty and must prevail, and it is hardly probable that any youth ever had this idea more firmly imbeded in his cranium than did I. I apparently moved in a different sphere while in her presence, and certainly did while all the little McGinnes' were around.

These trips across the country were usually made on horseback, and the terror that would overcome an individual under the circumstances above related, when learning that the faithful animal had broken loose and endeavored to keep better hours than his rider, left me behind to mourn his departure, can be imagined. Among all my numerous trips, however, this happened only once; but, oh, that once! It was enough for a lifetime, and now I do not need to seek very deep in memory's store house to bring forth the incident.

It was on one Sunday afternoon in autumn, I placed the saddle upon a young horse, a very nice one, too, which was the favorite with my father. The animal was feeling quite gay, and to do justice to all concerned, we might say the rider was about ditto. There was a school house about a mile beyond where McGinnis lived, and I was in the habit of attending Sunday school there in the afternoon and then stop at the place of attraction on my return. On this particular afternoon I visited this place, as was the custom, and after the meeting was out I loitered around for a short time with a number of other boys, and finally went quite a distance from the house with one of them; when returning the people had all departed, and likewise my horse, as he had broken loose. The timber was very dense around there and the undergrowth in places was so thick it would be impossible for a horse to get through with saddle and bridle on, without becoming entangled. My blood almost stood still for a moment, for I knew that while it was possible the horse would follow the road around and reach home in safety, it was not at all probable, for its natural inclination would be to start directly east, which was an impassable country under the circumstances. What would the man of the house at home say, and oh, golly, how could I ever make it around to see Jennie! It was simply hoping in the face of an inevitable fate, and should that pride of my father be found strangled in the woods, if discovered at all, I could only conjecture the consequences. It was almost sundown, three miles from home, two creeks to cross, horse to find, girl to see, and a mind so bewildered I could not tell how old I was.

I bid my friend a hurried good-night and started for home, endeavoring if possible to trace the horse, but as darkness was coming on, I did not dare remain in the woods on foot. I covered those three miles in an alarming short time, and reached home just at dusk; but to reach home was but to add woe to my misery.

My father usually kept some men around the place ·to assist in farm work, and besides, I had a brother that would find no greater delight than torturing me under such circumstances. It is needless to say that I sought the barn yard the very first move.   Father was at the house, and I did not break the news to him, and much to my surprise, the boys rather sympathized and looked upon my dilema from a standpoint of commiseration rather than jest.   This of course did nothing toward finding the horse, but helped to raise the cloud slightly, as I expected a great hurrah from them when they discovered my position.   A lost horse and a waiting girl!—where is the boy that could think of resting under these conditions? I immediately saddled another horse and ostensibly went to look for the lost one, but despite the terror brought upon me by the thought that the poor brute was possibly tangled up in the timber and at the point of death from strangulation, the thought of the girl reigned first, and ere I had proceeded a mile on my mission as horse seeker, the thought of her anxious, disappointed looks and waiting were more than I could bear, and I came to the conclusion, horse or no horse, I would go and see the girl, and did so.   I .tried to smooth my conscience over with the thought that all will be well in the morning and the lost be standing at the gate.   It was very late when I arrived, but the father of the 'generation had not yet decided upon retiring.   His tales seemed dreadfully dry to-night, and I was

figgity, but stuck it out, and after he had departed,
I broke the news to Jennie. She was considerably wrought up over my misfortune, whether from
real feeling for me or the horse, I could not say,
but she sympathized with me and of course advo-
cated the idea of "all would be well in the morning." After an hour of talking on different subjects, the horse question rather lost its grip upon
me and I lived in something like a state of enjoyment for awhile until after the night had reached
its summit by several minutes.

I had no more than reached the poor creature
that was to carry me home, after leaving the house,
than the thought broke forth afresh and with all
its former terror. There was no use, I could not
sleep in such a troubled state of mind, so resolved
to take a little scout around for the horse. It was
like looking for a lost child in London. The idea of
looking for a horse in two or three thousand acres
of timber, and that in the night; yet the hunting, in
a measure, satisfied a burning conscience. I kept
up the search until nearly daylight, and then went
home in despair, to find there nothing but disappointment again. I went to the house, and had
just placed my head on the place of rest, when
the family became aroused and began preparing
for the day.

There was no use dodging the issue any longer;
the news must now be spread before the old gentleman. I thought there was but two things to do;
one was to tell him and rush out and jump into

the well, or to get my brother to act as spokesman, after I had again started out to search for the lost treasure. I decided upon the latter; and by the time the sun had reached the height to be in full view I was on the road. Tom broke the news to the head of the family after he was sure I was out of reach, and then he sought the realms of the barn; in other words, a case of "flee from the wrath to come." It is not necessary to pen the words that fell from his lips when Tom had finished.

I scoured the woods, I thought completely, until about noon, but my efforts were as barren as the desert, and the loss of sleep, together with the worry, began to tell on me. It seemed I could hold out no longer, and I went home resolving to let come what might.

Upon reaching the gate I was almost completely exhausted. By this time, however, the wrath of my progenitor had somewhat subsided, and I approached him in such a meek, sneaking way, that he took pity on me and did not lecture me very severely, yet he did not say anything about my resting, but had Tom saddle another horse and accompany me, with instructions to seek until found. It was almost like placing a man in a state of exile, for it now began to dawn upon me there would be nothing more to eat until the horse was found, unless I went over to see Jennie; the pride which I possessed forbade me doing this.

Tom sympathized with me now, and after going for an hour or so we came to some thickets; it was impossible to proceed further on horseback, so I hitched my horse and placed my limber frame upon the ground. We agreed that should we find the object of our search, the fact was to be made known by a shout.

Such an effort as it was to walk, but I proceeded on and on, wandering hither and thither, until the sun was crawling considerably to the westward. What would we do should night again approach and the horse not found? I could never go home, and it was out of the question to remain there after dusk, as it was all one could do to get around in the daylight.

After having kept this up until just about ready to give up in despair, I heard Tom shout; the blood in my veins started afresh and I was changed in an instant, but then the thought flashed across my mind, dead or alive; if the former, what then?

I rushed toward the sound of his voice with all possible dispatch, and upon reaching him, you may imagine my surprise and delight to find everything all right, with the exception of a few broken straps. The horse had simply become entangled, and there waited patiently, or not exactly patiently either, as the ground gave evidence that all the waiting had not been as patient as it might have been, but it waited because it could not do otherwise.

I lost just as little time as possible after this until I had my feet under the table and was partaking of the luxuries of the land, with a clear conscience, but, I guess, a sneaking appearance.

After this, father McGinnis always took particular pains to see that my horse was placed in his barn during my stay there, and as practice makes perfect, I soon learned the crooks of his barn and could go in and get my animal without difficulty.

CHAPTER IV.

AMBITION AND ITS FRUITS.

A year or so passed without anything of much importance occurring, during which time I was attending school in winter and laboring on the farm in summer, forgetting what I had conquered in an intellectual line during the winter; but as most of the boys of my age there in the neighborhood did not even attend school in the winter, I was considered quite fortunate in this regard. All this time, too, my visits at the house of Jennie was as regular as of old. By this time I had become so familiar with all the family I could assist in the grand drag, at retiring time for the kids, with a good grace, and was only anxious for the approach of such time. The antique man had told me all the tales he knew five or six times, and every incident of his life from kidhood to old age, I think, but I had to swallow it all without a whimper, or at least, thought so.

About this time my ambition began to burst over its bounds, and I came to the conclusion I had been in the intellectual rut long enough, and that something must be done to give my cogitative powers more sway and a larger field, consequently

448401

it was decided that Jack be allowed to attend
school in a neighboring village during the winter.
Upon receiving assurance of this fact, I was apparently six inches taller and imagined that after a
short course in "town school," to cause a stag-
nation in the business world and grapple with
the mighty men of the earth would require but a
meagre effort on my part.   The village was only
about ten miles from home, but my back once
turned upon the drudgery of farm life, I was fairly well satisfied, for I little questioned but what I
was going to make my strike in life in a few
months at the longest.

The place was small, and the people a very
nice class of individuals.   But of course they
could at a glance penetrate my extreme greenness,
yet they sympathized with me and treated me
kindly, and I shall always remember the people
of Roxbury with kindness.   I soon became acquainted, had the rough edges knocked off little
by little, until in a few weeks I was enjoying life
very well and at the same time getting a little philosophy and cold mathematics impressed upon my
obtuse mind.   I studied a little occasionally when
the circumstances demanded, and usually had my
lessons as well as the average.

There was quite a large school, and, as would
naturally follow, there was quite a number of ideal
school girls, some of which I thought tolerably
nice, and the more I let this idea operate upon
me the more I became impressed with the fact

that there were really others of the fairer portion
of the race besides Jennie, and I did not seem to
like her as I used to; did not see her very often
and did not take occasion to write very promptly
after receiving her letters. That I treated her
real mean, would be about the proper expression.
When I occasionally went to see her during my
stay in town she would accuse me of inattention
regarding her, and insinuate that I was allowing
my copious affections to float in other directions.
Of course I would positively deny that I had ever
allowed any such thoughts to meander through
my rapidly developing brain; but the fact of the
matter was, I never seemed to care very much
for Jennie except while in her presence; and, as
Lew Wallace says, "There is no philosophy in such
love," etc.

It always pleased me to visit home about once
a month, sometimes a little oftener, and remain a
day or two and then return to school. On one of
these occasions, for the second time in my existence, I thought the time had arrived for me to
cross the golden gutter and render up an account
of my stewardship to the man at the gate.

It was customary for me to remain at home on
such visits during Saturday, and until Sunday
evening, and then return; but on this particular
date, on account of a severe snow storm, it was
decided I had better wait until the next day.
There were some neighboring boys that lived about
a mile from our home, and being very anxious to see

them, Tom and I resolved we would go over and call on them that evening.

We went on horseback, and I was perched upon the back of a fleet-footed animal, though young, and not familiar to carrying a passenger through a driving snow storm. The snow had drifted very deep in places, and it being so cold and disagreeable, we wished to abbreviate the time required to pass over the intervening space between home and the object of our mission, hence we were riding very rapidly, and in passing over the brow of a small hill, in starting down the incline, we ran right into a snow drift, and the horse which carried me stumbled and fell, throwing me completely over his head, and I struck on my back in the snow. The fall did not hurt me much, the snow being very light, but the animal was frightened and in floundering around to get up, struck me squarely in the face with his front foot. Talk about astronomy, but I think the stars I saw would fully equal the number of the whole universe, and but from the fact that the horse had no shoe on, I would, beyond a doubt, there and then, have joined the silent majority. As it was, the snow being soft, my head gave way easily and the hoof of the animal slipped off, not, however, without having taken considerable of the cuticle from my face. Fright, pain and cold together wrought upon me to such an extent that I did not know whether to conclude I was sure enough dead, or whether I should get up. Tom came to my rescue and picked up what there was left of me, but when he saw the disfigured condition of my features he was considerably excited. Acting upon first impulse, he tied our handkerchiefs around my face, recaptured the horses and we turned homeward, being then about half a mile from home. Upon reaching the house I was a frightful looking sight, the blood having run down and frozen in all sorts of shapes on my face; this, together with the handkerchief blurring it around, caused me to resemble an inhabitant of the morgue. Poor mother was frightened half to death, but true to a mother's nature, she soon had my face washed and bandaged as best she could and my dilapidated form placed in bed. By receiving kind treatment and the very best possible care, I was soon able to be up, and in the course of a week or so went back to school, although the wounds were not yet all healed up; time, however, placed my face in about as respectable a condition as ever, with the exception of one or two small scars which were stamped there for life.

Circumstances under which I was placed while attending school here, brought me in contact with a people that had a tendency somewhat to change my life to a certain extent morally, and despite boyish hilarity and fun, which is natural in a human, I felt the need of something a little different, a little more peace of mind. In other words, I awoke to the fact that man has interests other than those that are material; he has aspirations that sweep beyond time and this world; he is more than his body; he is greater than his life; he has a vision that is not of the eye; he has within, a "still small voice" that compels attention now and then. We are apt to forget these things in this whirling age and country. Most of us are utterly immersed in worldy pursuits and wholly occupied with selfish struggles, so that the moral part of our nature is wholly neglected. I do not say that people should not improve their material fortunes, but still there is something else that must not be overlooked. There is a moral nature, the neglect of which means moral death.

When the pulse beats high and we are flushed with youth and health and vigor, when all goes on prosperously, and success seems almost to anticipate our wishes, then we feel not the want of the consolation of a religion; but when fortune frowns, or friends forsake us, when sorrow or sickness comes upon us, then it is that the superiority of the pleasure of religion is established over those of dissipation and vanity, which are ever apt to fly from us when we are most in want of their aid. The man who believes there is no God, no immortality, and that when he dies he will melt into the earth to be seen no more, like the snow flake sinking into the ocean, certainly wants one of the most wonderful stimulants to intellectual and moral advancement.

Weary human nature lays its head on the bosom of the Divine Word, or it has no where to lay its head. Tremblers on the verge of the dark and terrible valley which parts the land of the living from the untried hereafter, take this hand of human tenderness, yet of God-like strength, or they totter into the gloom without stop or stay. I had at times been considering life from a moral standpoint, but to me religion seemed very strange, things had changed very materially since the ushering in the Christian era, and the question was, If Christ had been the real Christ, as was claimed, and had established his church, as we are told he did, who had the right to change it? That the mode of procedure was different than 1800 years before, must be noticeable to even the casual observer; hence, when I found a people that were worshiping under the system established according to the Holy Writ, I united with them, and I cannot say that I have ever repented that act; in fact, am satisfied it was one proper step of my life. This did not, as many seem to think it does, lessen the pleasure of life in the least. I was naturally endowed with a desire to have sport, and when any practical joking was going on, my name might always be figured in the list, and sometimes such action has caused me more or less trouble.

One instance I remember particularly, which occurred along in the Spring, while I was yet attending school there, and it came near proving serious. Pete Brown, a fellow that boarded at the same place I did, and I went down to the express

office one evening after dark to get a valuable
package. We noticed as we passed the railroad
depot that there was one of those three-wheeled
railroad tricycles sitting there, which was naturally very tempting to us. We proceeded to the express office, secured the package and was returning; but on again reaching the depot, the tricycle
still sitting there, we could not resist the temptation. The agent was in the office, and the tricycle
belonged to a friend of his, that was also in the
office, having run down from a neighboring station
for a visit. They were talking and laughing, and
without further preliminaries, we threw the package
into an empty box-car, pulled the wheeled machine
out onto the track, and both got on. It moved
off so nicely we were delighted, and before we had
gone half a mile it seemed out of the question to
turn around, so we kept on going. After getting
out a mile or two, the idea struck us to proceed to
the next town, which we did.

Whatever prompted us to do such a thing I cannot now imagine, but all thoughts of the package
and the forlorn box-car were forgotten. After
going several miles, the novelty of the business
began to wear off, but we pressed on until we
reached the point we started for. Then came the
return, which was not near so pleasant. We kept
changing off, one working the handles awhile and
then the other, but it was very evident that it was
getting far into the night, and the changes more
frequent every mile, and besides we were cold.

By this time we commenced to regret our adventure, and wish we were at home in bed; however, by persistent effort we reached the town about midnight, and then the thought of the package began to dawn upon us. The depot was locked up, and every one gone, and on going to the box-car where we had deposited our treasure, our hearts almost ceased to beat, * * * it was gone. What could we do or say to claim the package! if taken by the agent, would but be to give the snap away, and if stolen, what should we do, as we were cautioned to be careful with it. Although we searched and searched for the lost package, it was worse than folly, and finally went home sadder but much wiser. What could we tell the folks that had sent us for the package? Scheme as we might, there seemed to be no outlet, unless the package was cheap enough that we could afford to duplicate it.

Next morning we answered the call for breakfast, looking about as sneaking as it is possible for any one with a human face to look, and feeling, if it were possible, even worse than we looked. There was nothing under the sun that we could do but explain; the expressman held our receipt for the package and there was no use to deny getting it. We told the whole truth about the matter, and "we were sick of our job," and all that; but that did not replace the package, and upon inquiry we found it far more valuable than our limited funds could stand to replace. There was

yet but one hope, and that was, the young lady
that had sent us for the package was a very intimate friend of the agent, and we appealed to her.
I presume now she wished to teach us a lesson,
for she did not give us much satisfaction, but
nevertheless I am confident she went and had an
interview with the station agent, when we were
not aware of it, for we were informed, though not
directly, that the agent had the package. She
insisted that we go and ask him for it, which,
after waiting all day, we reluctantly complied
with her request. The agent was wrathy, and
we were frightened. He cornered us up and
made us confess that we took the wheel, which
did not belong to us, and he further informed
us that the wheel was broken; in short, he gave
us such a talk that the hair was standing almost perpendicular on our heads when we sneaked
out of the depot without the package. He demanded much more money than we could pay,
and besides, threatened to have us arrested. We
told the man we were boarding with, he took the
matter in hand, and finally we allowed it to run
along until it was in the hands of the marshal,
when a compromise was effected by our paying a
certain amount. We then breathed natural again
for the first time in two or three days. This is one
of the most valuable lessons I have ever learned,
and it has stuck to me thus far through life, and
I believe, though I should live to count many
and many moons yet, I would never be accused
of taking what did not belong to me, even for
sport, where such serious trouble might result.

CHAPTER V.

Summer soon came now, and instead of rush-ing out and surprising the civilized world by my startling maneuvers, I was forced to return to the farm. Oh, but it was tough to go to work again, those long, hot spring days, after living in town and doing but little. It was so much harder to work than it had been before, but time wore things back into their usual channel, and life was something as it had been in other days. Being forced to return to the farm, my city pride left me, and I again began to visit the McGinnis ranch, with as much pleasure, or nearly so, as of old. Soon after my return from school, however, an incident took place which cast a shadow over my life, a shadow which can never be raised.

Though it was but what is inevitable in human existence, yet we were wholly unprepared on this occasion. The cause of the trouble was that the death angel entered the family and claimed one of its inmates. What a strange occurrence it is, to be sure, and while it is sometimes so sudden and un-expected, sometimes lingering for years at the very threshold, yet the wise men of our land are unable to solve its mysteries. One of our writers once said, in writing on this subject: "Life is a journey; the end is nearing when the still monster is wont to approach. Life is a race, the goal will soon be reached; it is a voyage, the port will soon be in sight; are we not justifiable in saying, time is but a narrow isthmus between two extremes; we are all going. How many things you have already left behind!—the old home, friends, parents, scenes of childhood and early years! How much of the way you have passed over! You will never return to the place from whence you started! You are going on and on, always from your early years! It is a startling thought that our business will soon be left behind; that our work will soon be done, and that we shall leave this stage of being—leave it forever,—our homes and cares, and all the interests that engage us here, and never, never more come back in this condition again."

In meditating upon this thought we call to mind another quotation on the same subject, which reads: "Life is like a summer's residence at a bathing place. When you arrive, you first become acquainted with those who have been there for some weeks, and who leave you in a few days. This separation is painful. Then you turn your attention to those who arrived with you. With them you live a good while and become really intimate. But soon the most of these go also, and you are left lonely with those that came about the time you were going away. You have but little to do with them. Some stay long, some but a short time in this world. Some souls blossom almost as soon as they enter this life, and then they depart. The flower that opens when it breaks from the ground, and then dies, is an emblem of the infant that dies. Violets are the children and youth who finish their mission near life's entrance and then depart.

"But every life, no matter how short, accomplishes something. An infant, a prattling child, dying in its cradle, will live again in the better thoughts of those who loved it, and play its part, through them, in the redeeming actions of the world, though its body be burned to ashes or drowned in the deepest sea. There is not an angel added to the host of heaven, but does its blessed work on earth, in those that loved it here. Oh, if the good deeds of human creatures could be traced to their source, how beautiful would even death appear! How much charity, mercy and purified affections would be seen to arise from beds of death!

"When death strikes down the innocent and young, to every fragile form from which he lets the panting spirit free, a hundred virtues arise in shapes of mercy, charity and love, to walk the world and bless it. Of every tear that sorrowing mortals shed on such green graves, some good is born, some gentler nature comes. In the destroyer's steps there springs up bright creations that defy his power, and his dark path becomes a way

of light to heaven. There is nothing in all the
earth that we can do for the dead. They do
not need us, but we forever and forever more need
them."

What a memorable epoch in the history of a
home is that in which death finds his first entrance
within its sacred inclosures, and with ruthless
hand, breaks the first link of a golden chain that
creates its identity! That event is never forgotten. It may be the first born, in the radiant beauty
of youth, or the babe in the first bursting of life's
budding loveliness, or a father in the midst of his
anxious cares, or the mother who gave light and
happiness to all around her,—whoever it is, the
first death makes a breach there which no subse-
quent bereavement can equal. New feelings are
then awakened; a new order of associates is then
commenced; hopes and fears are then aroused that
never subside, and the mysterious web of family
life receives the hue of a new and darker thread.

Most of us have stood and wrung our hands at
parting with some one who will never more
come back to us in this world, but such partings
and memories are not wholly in vain. There are
things back of us, known only to heaven, which
have greatly shaped our lives. There are faces,
and the pressure of hands, and snatches of song,
and the light of long closed eyes, and the far distant murmur of solemn prayer, which we treasure evermore. There ARE those with faith enough
to think that by and by the old faces will be seen

once more, the loved voices heard anew, and all
the lost ones will be once more found, but here
the horrible shadow of doubt flashes across my
mind, and I am lost in its mysteries.

The flower fadeth, but the seed and the fruit
remain; and this teaches us there is nothing to
sadden us in the process of decay in nature and
vegetation. This is preliminary to a higher growth.
Our present life, with all its activities and enjoyments, is but the flower form of a being whose
fruit form is found in an after and higher life, and
decay and death are no more than the falling of
petals from the well-set fruit.

Of all the solemnities of which the mind can
conceive, death is the greatest. There may be,
here and there, an empty heart and a thoughtless
brain, across which no meditations pass for months,
or even years; but these are exceptional characters,
and leave unaffected the truth that no reflection
comes to man with such uniformity and power as
the thought that, in a few years, we shall all be
far away. That which is thus universal must be
for the common good. Death comes equally to
all, and makes us all equal when he comes. The
ashes of an oak in the chimney are no epitaph of
the tree; it tells us not how high it was, how large
it was, or what flocks it sheltered while it stood.
The fate which overtook that tree is a fit emblem
of death, which, in its restless course, levels alike
the king and the peasant, the wise and the ignorant, the rich and the poor, the old and the young.

This world is the subdued and vested domain of death. The history of the past is a record of the triumph of the king of terrors. In all lands the generation of the departed outnumber the living, and all that now live must soon taste death. There is no pathway of life where the destroyer may not be met at any moment. There is no home from which the grim shadow of death can be shut out. The bloom of youth, the strength of manhood, the glory of age, are withered in his icy breath, as the late flowers wither in the frost of autumn.

But if this be the gateway to future good, why should we dread it? Were we deprived of all hopes of a future existence, still constituted as we are, to the great majority of us, the time must come when even annihilation would be preferable to continued existence. Could we always live young, in the possession of health, strength and friends, the case might be different; but age and infirmities will be our lot, the heart will grow weary and we long for rest.

In all the returns and gatherings of earth there are some missing. Many times the lost are more than the found. The further we go on the journey of life, the fewer of the friends of youth are left to keep us company. When we visit a former home after a long absence, and enquire for the friends of other years, we are told of one and another that they have gone the way whence they will not return. And, as time passes on, we are

all getting more names for the roll of our acquaintances, whose places are vacant, who gather with
us no more, who answer not when their names are
called. The crowd presses on with hurried and
heedless tread in the very path out of which men
are constantly passing from time into eternity,
sometimes at a single step.

The flame of life burns so feebly upon the secret
altar of the heart that it can be put out by a sudden jar or a single breath. The partition between
us and the unseen world is as thin as the garments
that clothe our flesh, and as easily pierced as the
bubbles that float on the waves. As life is thus
critical, any word may be our last, any farewell,
even amid glee and merriment, may be forever.
If this truth were but burned into our consciousness, would it not give a new meaning to all our
human relationship? How much more kindness
would there be in the world were this thought acted
upon.

Human friends may go hand in hand to the very
brink of the cold river that rolls between this and
the unseen land. They may do much to soothe
and sustain each other as the last hour draws near.
But there is a point beyond which human help
cannot go. Every one of us must advance to
meet the great and final foe, with no human hand
on which to lean. We must turn away our faces
from our earthly friends, and pass in under the
deep shadow of eternity without their company.

Each individual must stand exposed to the dread arrow of the great destroyer, with none to turn aside the shaft.

We believe that life was made to be enjoyed, and he who would dampen all pleasures, with mournful reflections on the. fleeting nature of earthly enjoyments, displays but little wisdom, to say the least. But still there are times when, as reasonable creatures, it becomes us to contemplate that solemn moment when for the soul, time ends and eternity begins. Our friends may stretch out their hands to keep us back, but no entreaties on their part can change the course. of events. They might offer large retainers, but death accepts no fee. The breath will fail, the eyes will close, the heart will cease to beat. · You may hang the couch with gorgeous· tapistry, but death respects no finery.

We, as a multitude, are hurrying along; we are chained to the chariot of revolving time; there is no bridling the steed nor leaping from the chariot, and some are even so burdened with the sorrows of life, that they rashly invoke the presence of the death angel, and of their own will, lay aside the robes of flesh.

Life, no doubt, should be a scene of happiness; but largely from our own fault, it is true, all know that it abounds with many trying scenes. Wonderful is the power of death to disarm resentment, to kindle anew the fires of love and friendship in the heart. When the veil has been drawn be-

:tween us and the object of our regard, how quick
sighted do we become to their merits, and how
bitterly do we remember words, or even looks, of
unkindness, which may have escaped in our inter-
course with them. How .careful should such
thoughts render us in the fulfillment of offices of
affection which may yet be in our power to perform! Who can tell how soon the moment may
arise when repentance cannot be followed by rep-
aration! Probably, if we were to think more upon
this subject, not in a somber, melancholy sort of
way, but as becomes rational beings, we would do
many things differently than we do at present."

'Twas the first time I had ever known real sorrow, and for this reason, among others, I was not
fully prepared for what took place. My oldest
sister, Nellie, was several years my senior, and
had been the one I was wont to acquaint with my
minor troubles, and when in doubt I always went
to her, and, although she had been married for a
number of years, her home was not far from ours,
and, regardless of how busy she might be with
the affairs of life, she always had a willingness to
listen to my difficulties, and never failed to have
words of comfort and encouragement to offer. In
short, she had almost spoiled me. I would not
think of taking up a study without first consulting
her, and no matter what my opinion might have
been, her decision, with me, was final. I acted
upon her advice, and though many years have now
passed since she crossed over to the other shore,

I wish I might be able to council with her yet, get advice from her and profit thereby. Had she lived, no doubt my life would have been different, my career would have been less checkered, and my existence more pleasant.

The remark is common, that death always seems to call upon the best first, and while we sometimes hear this questioned, I hardly think it could have been in this case, at least it was not with me. Sometimes, immediately following her death, I would find myself lost in meditation, trying to solve the mysteries connected with death, and why could not some one else have been taken in her place. I felt that I would have willingly acted as a substitute, but the angel that brought the message did not leave it to our option, nor did he question us as to who should answer the summons. When thinking over it, for perhaps an hour, and having reached the maximum of my meditative powers, I would find myself driven completely to the wall, and with bewildered thoughts I could but exclaim, My God, where is the justice in this!

She was only sick a few days, but despite every effort that kind hands or loving hearts could do, even the medical skill of the age, she gradually grew worse. Hope as we might, it all seemed purely in vain, and when for a time we imagined the worst was over, it afterwards transpired that death was but withholding his stern hand apparently to increase our burning anxiety. Living and hoping under such circumstances soon becomes terrible, at least so it was with me, for I do not believe it is possible for the feeling between sister and brother to be stronger than was the feeling that existed between Nellie and I. Finally we were forbidden to go into the room; it was only then that I began to realize that the worst was at hand, and the thought that I must never see her again in her rational mind, seemed almost unbearable. All the afternoon we lived in this awful suspense, then night came, and with it a terrible storm; it really seemed that the death angel had combined with the elements to make our existence as terrible as it could be. The blinding lightning, the horrible peals of thunder, and the rush and roar of the driving hail and rain, caused an uncommon and frightening noise, but it disturbed not the pale face and quiet form upon the couch that was so soon to be the scene of death. All hope of her reviving was at last given up, and the family permitted to gather around her. What then followed is as fresh in my memory as though it were but a few months ago, instead of years. The fact was only too evident that life was taking its departure; it seemed my blood stood still, I could not realize that the surrounding circumstances were a reality. She spoke a few words of advice, addressing them more particularly to mother, then one last, longing look at her husband, and all was over. The rain still continued to beat against the side of the house, the lightning flashed and the thunder continued its terrible peals, but it had a different sound to us now. I do not believe it is within the power of even death to strike a harder blow than this was, when we fully realized that all earthly hope had vanished. From that hour I was different; I have never looked upon life in exactly the same light since. And even now, sometimes when sitting alone in my room, when the storm is howling without, my mind runs back through all these years, and I think of a little mound, in a lonely place, many miles away, and before I am aware of the fact, I discover a silent tear stealing down my cheek, in reverence to that thought.

CHAPTER VI.

In the State of Iowa, located on one of its beautiful, rolling prairies, stands the little town of
Hardstudy. From every point of compass the surrounding country is beautiful to behold. The inhabitants, about three thousand in number, were
of the middle class, honest, or at least, claimed
to be, most of them energetic, and hence had a
thriving little village. In the eastern part of the
little burg, located on a slight elevation, stood a
college building, with a capacity of accommodating
about seven or eight hundred green country boys
and girls each year, for the purpose of having
their intellectual faculties brushed up a little, preparing them, as most of them presumed when
they went there, for coming statesmen or world-
startlers. From the glowing advertisements that
had flooded the country for two or three hundred
miles around, in every direction, most of those
attending, presumed that education was hanging
around on bushes, and all a fellow had to do was
to pay his money, pick up an education, have
some fun, and spring into life's arena fully equipped

to meet its stern realities. Some who went with these expectations, left a few months later, poorer, sadder and wiser.

As stated in the previous chapter, I earned bread by the sweat of my brow during the coming summer, after having attended school in the village near home. My aspirations had been so completely mangled; I resolved this time I would make a strike for life, so decided I would study shorthand for life or death. I had my eye on the above mentioned place, and after considerable corresponding with the professor of the shorthand department, resolved to cast my anchor there as soon as the work on the farm would permit, and then and there tangle my brain up with the mysteries of the art. The opening of our story relates what took place when I broke the news to the head of the family. It did not take a Philadelphia lawyer to discover from his actions that he was not particularly anxious that I should pursue this course of study, and in fact discouraged it in every way possible; but I had been studying over the subject of "farm or starve," for so long, that I had about concluded to take chances on the latter before engage in agricultural pursuits another year. One of the greatest drawbacks to a farmer boy when living at home is, he never sees very much of the surplus finance, if it ever happens there is any. He can work and work, raise crops, stock and pumpkins, sell them for a good price, but what good does it do him? The farm is car-

ried on under the co-operative system, the head
of the house president, secretary and treasurer,
and the boys the employees; or, to give it a more
modern expression, would say, he is the grindee
of the monopoly.   His remuneration consists of
his board and clothes, the latter depending very
materially upon the success of the bean and pump-
kin crop.   Of course times were exceedingly hard,
as they always are, or at least always have been
since I was old enough to remember; but as the
fall months began to come, arrangements were
planned to give me one more push into the world.
With this thought in mind I worked hard, for I
had determined it would be the last work I should
do on the place that I had labored on all my life.
Thus far in life it has been, but during some discouraging times which I have encountered since
then, I have thought my complaints were not
altogether well founded.

Tom and I had many pleasant times there, and,
as is the case with every human being who will,
we had our associates.   I might here casually
mention that about this time, Jennie and I had a
"scrap," which resulted in a discontinuation of
my visits to the McGinnis ranch for some time
previous to my leaving home.   Like most kids
do, we "parted forever," but as friends; however,
I did not meet her in conversation after that before our departure.

The folks did not like to see me go, especially
mother, for while I had not positively asserted that

I was turning my back upon the farm, everything went to show that such were my intentions. Everyone knows what the preliminaries are prior to one's starting to school; mine was no exception; if anything, it was worse than the average.

There were two or three going to Hardstudy from the neighboring village where I had attended school the previous winter, about the same time I did, so we partially arranged to go together. One fellow named Samuel Tough had arranged to occupy the same room with me when we reached the place, but owing to circumstances he left one day before I did.

Sunday morning father took me to the village, from which I was to start the next day for Hardstudy. One of my girl acquaintances was going at the same time also, hence we arranged matters accordingly. As tired as I was of farm life, it was not an easy matter to leave, under the circumstances, but being of a superstitious character regarding looking back, when once started, I kept my face straight forward.

We were to take the train at an early hour next morning, two or three hours before day, but the train was late and we waited a long time. After going about sixty miles we reached the point where we were to change cars and take another road, but we had missed connections. Neither of us had ever traveled any, and there was nothing but freight trains until the next day. 'Twas a shabby little place, and nothing to interest one at all, so we resolved not to remain over night in the place. There was a through freight coming along about dusk that night, and for the want of better judgment we decided to take that. We did, and we were extremely sorry; reached Hardstudy about two o'clock in the morning and walked a mile or more to a hotel, found they only had room for one, so I went on by myself to another place.

Next morning about nine o'clock I meandered out to find the object of my search, the school building. About half a mile out, I beheld what was to be my place of existence for a few months, the exact time I did not know. I did not seem to have taken into consideration that there was a tremendous lot of hard studying connected with shorthand. I was thinking more of having a good time and then, starting in life for myself.

Once in life fortune favored me, for the first person I struck was Sam Tough; he had been there and taken in the situation and knew the lay of the land. When I left for the place I had quite a wad of ducats, the most I had ever had at one time in my life, and I guarded it with an eagle eye, for I was not sure where the next was to come from. Sam had arranged to board in the building, so of course I should do the same. The first pass he took me into the proprietor's office and told him I wanted board for a term. "Twenty dollars," says Mr. Proprietor, and I grasped the wad, paid him and got my receipt. Then we went to look for the shorthand "boss," told him my errand. Thirty-five dollars for first term, and I paid him. He also gave me a list of books I was to get, which I immediately proceeded to obtain. Room to pay for, and coal to buy! my, how my currency was melting! It was very evident they understood that much of their business, viz: get the bulk of a fellow's pile before he had time to spend it down town.

Sam had been on track of a room, but all he could turn up was a dirty room in a building called "The Students' Home." The words had a sort of soothing influence, but they were as full of deceit as an egg is full of meat. It was a square building containing twelve rooms, each room supposed to be occupied by two students, making twenty-four of us in the building, but it was an awful desolate place. The rooms were like stalls in a barn, still, they answered the purpose, and rooms were very scarce, for the school was large and the town small. Sam said it was the best we could do now, so we engaged it for one term. We had the northwest room on the ground floor, the worst room in the building, and as cold as a summer kitchen; but, nevertheless, we moved in and entered upon our new sphere of existence, for such it might well be called. Imagine twenty-four boys in a building nearly a quarter of a mile from the college, no one to watch them. To tell the story in a few words, it was never quiet.

In the afternoon of the first day, I went up and made my start at shorthand, commencing of course, on the alphabet. It did not take long to learn it, but my fingers were so stiff from hard work, and my brain so inactive and obtuse that I made very slow progress when it came to speed. The master of ceremonies told me it would be necessary for me to learn to write the alphabet at least three times per minute before going any further. I did not do much the first afternoon, but learn the alphabet; next morning, I went up, made the letters satisfactory and then went home, or to the "den," as we commonly called it, and began working up my speed. I worked tolerably well until along in the afternoon; I thought I was getting in pretty fair shape, and imagined I would be a court reporter in a few weeks. There was no question in my own mind but what my success warranted the impression that I was doing fine, and my aspirations broke forth afresh. About 4 p. m., with the dignity and confidence in self, presumably possessed by a military officer, I proceeded to the place of trial. The man at the helm of the shorthand department took me into a room by myself, placed me in a chair, took out his watch and said, Go! I went, but owing to the state of excitement under which I was laboring, it seemed the wheels of intellect were locked, and those bruised up fingers refused to get in their work. Time was called, minute up, perspiration running down my forehead, and there before me lay the paper with the most outlandish looking scrawls thereon that human-eyes ever witnessed, when they had been made with the intention of being anything of an intelligent nature. I had worried about one and a half times over the alphabet. He looked disappointed, and I know I felt that way; he suggested that perhaps I was a little excited, had better try again. We took another turn for sixty seconds; this time resulted a little better than the time before, but nothing near three times per minute, so there was nothing to do but to return to the den, and once more enter into secret deliberation, with a view of becoming more accustomed to the peculiarities of the art.

I have since learned, many times, that the excitement and failure made at that time was but a foretaste of what a stenographer must experience in this very regard. Excitement of the body materially retards quick action of the brain, and for this very reason a great many stenographers, just starting out, make a failure on their initiatory trial for a position. To do good work, and write rapidly, one must be perfectly composed, regardless of the surrounding circumstances, and, if there is ever a time when we must have an abundance of self-confidence, self-will and determination, it is when we are on a trial of this kind.

By the next morning, continued effort had succeeded in getting up a more direct line of connection between brain and fingers, and once more entering the private chamber of his royal highness, succeeded in crossing the three times per minute line, and was given some further principles to digest. After having, in a manner, conquered them, I was started in the primer, and given a page to transcribe from long hand to shorthand, using what principles that had been introduced. If memory proves true, this was about the third day after our advent to the place, and new landmarks becoming somewhat familiar, working over a desk became a little more pleasant, and the crooked marks were slowly making an impression on the inner portion of my skull. I prepared the transcript, and thought it in pretty fair shape, being very careful in the preparation of same, but upon going up to have it corrected, the corrections being made with red ink, it was hard to tell, after he had finished working with it, which was the original, the red marks or the black, they were about equal in number. This made me feel discouraged, but I tried again, taking even more pains this time than at fiast, but the red ink pen made another desperate slaughter, and I went home disappointed, discouraged and home-sick. I had about come to the conclusion I could never be a shorthand writer anyway, and wished I had never come there. As the close of the day was approaching. I would wonder how Tom was getting along, if mother was sorry I had left home, if the cows were all at home, where the old farm dog was, and all this, until I felt as though farming was not so bad after all.

It is never all bad without a little good, and Sam was one of those jolly fellows that rarely ever became discouraged, and his presence assisted very materially in arousing my down-trodden feelings.

CHAPTER VII.

Sam was endeavoring to master what was there called the "commercial course," consisting of book-keeping, penmanship, etc., but he did not at all take kindly to study; in fact the only thing he cared much about was sport, and he had fully his share of that. He was very rusty in mathematics, miserable penman, and butchered orthography up in the most cruel and outrageous manner; under these circumstances, I thought if he could ever become an efficient book-keeper, I should certainly be able to make at least an apology for a stenographer. We arranged that we should alternately rise first in the morning and kindle the fire; this plan worked very well for a time. After awhile Sam seemed to be experiencing an enormous amount of difficulty with the mathematical part of his studies, so we agreed that when it came my morning to manufacture a fire, we would both arise at once, and while he did the necessary with the stove, I would solve some of his perplexing mathematical stringencies. Under this regime at the den, we labored for some time.

After a few days of having my work scraped over with the read ink pen, I began to get onto the racket a little, and was, in the course of about a week, introduced to the type-writer. Strange it may seem, I took much more kindly to this, and experienced very little difficulty, other than missing about half of the words when attempting to spell them correctly; this trouble, however, I was informed that most every one encountered when starting. Then I entered the primary class and commenced to take dictation, and here is where I made one of the worst blunders with the work. I imagined that I must write just as rapidly as the others, whether I should ever be able to read it or not; but every stenographer who has ever had an extended experience can readily understand the error in this. I am inclined to believe that a great many make a mistake in this, when entering a class that has a few weeks the start of them, to endeavor to be up with the best of them, laboring under the impression that time will teach them to read their notes readily, but a sadder mistake could never be made by a stenographic aspirant. The same principle will hold good in typewriting as well as shorthand; be accurate, get what you do get so you can read it, and speed will come of its own accord. I did not invest much time in reading my notes, but studied some on the principles, some on orthography, practiced penmanship a little and commenced to get acquainted with the boys, the latter occupying

much more of my time than it should. While
there is no question but what fun is all right in its
place, even while one is attending school, yet I
am now convinced, and was at the end of three
months, that I had invested entirely too much
time in sport.

Sam was a handsome young fellow, dressed much
better than the average student at such a school,
and of course, the girls there, as a great many of
them do everywhere, judge a man principally
by his clothes. Near the college building stood a
large dormitory, the ground floor being occupied
by girls and the upper floor by boys. It was
against the rules of the establishment for the boys
to visit the lower rooms after six o'clock, but Sam
was not to be baffled by a little thing like this.
In the corner room there were two girls, one of
them what we might term real pretty, the other one
only moderate, but that Sam was very favorably impressed with one of them was evident from his
actions when he passed the room, and from her
copious smiles, it was equally as true she believed
in reciprocity in this regard. What an elegant
opportunity to play a practical joke! I could not
let it pass; so getting a fellow to write in a fine
hand, something similar to the handwriting of a
lady, I fixed up the note and addressed it to Sam,
signing it in such a manner that he would know,
or think, at least, that it was written by the girl
in the corner room, and invited him to call that
afternoon, it being Saturday. The note was prompt-

ly mailed, and equally as promptly received by
Sam, as he was usually loitering around town Sat-
urdays.   He bit without a kick, never mistrusted
anything, and did not awake to the fact that he
had been the subject of a joke, until informed
direct by the object of the visit, but the girl was
not at all displeased with his visit and they became acquainted, yet to this day neither of them,
to my knowledge, knows who the author of the
note was.   Sam did not want to leave at six, but
did, I presume, with the understanding that he
would call around later and stand and talk through
the open window.   Whether this arrangement had
been previously agreed upon or not, I cannat say,
but that he did so stand and talk, I can vouch
for.   Curiosity led me to act as a spy that evening, and see where he went after leaving the den;
this I did, and soon discovered him leaning into
the window of the corner room, very busily engaged in conversation with the inmates.   His
elbows were on the window sill and he was standing
in a very comfortable position, entirely too much
so for me to resist the inviting temptation.   Being
acquainted with the fellows in the room directly
over him, running to the back entrance I gained
the room directly above where he was standing,
and then informed the boys of the circumstances
that were taking place below, asking for some
water.   This was furnished without hesitation,
the window quietly raised, and I then and there
treated Sam to a cold water bath.   'Twas a little

mean, but the deed was done; I knew he would be mad, and was aware of the fact that it would be policy for me to reach home before he did, if possible. After obtaining a promise that they would not give it away, took my departure via. the same route I had entered, and made all possible haste for the den. It appeared that Sam had not lingered to say many parting words, nor had he stopped by the wayside on his return home to count stars or listen to the warble of birds, for upon reaching the door, the noise from within was entirely too audible to permit doubt as to his' being there.

To say that he was wrathy, would be placing it in its mildest form; he was pacing up and down the room, gritting his teeth and talking as though he would thrash every fellow on the second floor of the dormitory, to be sure and get the right one. I professed perfect ignorance of the affair, and expressed surprise that any one should be guilty of so rude an act; but all efforts to pacify him proved in vain; nothing short of whipping the fellow that threw the water, would ever appease his wrath. A change of the subject and shortly the arrival of bed-time, quieted him for the evening, and the next morning he had partially outgrown it, although it would not have been policy for me to have allowed him to discover who the guilty party was. Of course, the boys who inhabited the room from whence the water came, gave nothing away.

On the date of the above occurrence, I formed
the acquaintance of one Oscar Jones, which has
proved to be a friendship of more than ordinary
nature. We seemed congenial from the very first,
and from that time on, our inclination toward each
other grew, and now the ties of friendship rarely
ever bind man and man nearer together than he
and I. Our friendship ripened very quickly, and
well that it did, for a few days after that, Oscar
was taken very sick. He was rooming in one of
the dormitories, in a sort of a pig-pen place, such
as was furnished the boys, and it was all a well
man could do to live in one of them, but when
sickness came, it was indeed tough. The household goods consisted of the bare absolute neces-
sities, that one might exist—a water pail and tin
cup constituted all the articles that you could use
to dish up anything in, for a sick person. His
sickness came near proving serious; he grew worse
rapidly and we called for the doctor; yet, to have
the doctor come, was but to add embarrassment
to his already wounded feelings, for there was
nothing to mix medicine in, save the tin cup, or
the full grown water pail. We gave him the cup,
which, proportionately, was equal to the widow's
mite; he mixed some sort of stuff therein, pur-
ported to be an antidote for sickness,, leaving
orders to give so. many teaspoonfuls, so often.
I could think of no better way than that he take
up the cup and drink until he thought about a
dose had been taken, but poor Oscar had never

been accustomed to such treatment, and could not entertain the idea of so administering the bitter drugs. After some preliminaries, we succeeded in getting a spoon and a glass; with these we were quite well fixed for taking care of the sick. His sickness lingered for several days, during which time I remained with him most of the time, except when I was engaged in stretching my intellect. Soon after his recovery from sickness, he secured a position in a wholesale dry goods house in the city of Gentleburg, and we were forced to part, not forever, however, as after years brought us together again.

The typewriter never failed to interest me, but to say that shorthand was a pleasant study, I could not conscientiously do so. One trouble being with my shorthand, I did not take pride enough in causing my notes to look neat, and getting them accurate, hence they were not so easily read as they might have been, had more pains been taken in placing them on the paper. Another thing that bothered me some, I did not fully master the principles before commencing to write, and had it not been for the one notable characteristic of my life, viz: to hang on as long as there is hope, I fear I should have given it up in despair, before having mastered the preface, as it were.

Soon after Oscar left school, Sam became too high-toned for the room we were in, and left me, having found an associate more congenial, and a far more pleasant room, thus I was left alone; and this, together with the loss of Oscar, caused me to feel lonesome for a time; but while alone, I could study more, and did so, and had the surroundings been anything like a human habitation, life might have been more pleasant. This lasted but a short time, however, as the term for which the room had been engaged, expired; 'tis needless to say I vacated it. After a little skirmishing around, secured a room with three other fellows, with a private family, a perfect palace, compared with the one I had been stopping in heretofore. The room was a very large one, and four of us could get along quite comfortably; the other three being of an amicable disposition, we studied in earnest.

Soon, I awoke to the fact that I was a little rusty in other branches besides shorthand, so commenced to study other branches, but all the time giving shorthand the preference. Soon after changing my place of habitation, the currency which I had brought from home became almost extinct, and as per agreement with the head of the family, I was to raise the necessary wherewith, so long as I attended school thereafter. I had already arranged with my brother, whose headquarters were in Butchertown, to loan me the money as he could spare it, so wrote him the circumstances, and received some currency, which placed me on my feet again, financially.

Six or eight months prior to this, there had been quite a serious shooting afray in Hardstudy, in which two or three lives were lost. The shorthand professor had attended the preliminary trial and taken the evidence, which he preserved and had it dictated to the class. They dictated from this testimony about one hour each day. While taking this, I first became interested in shorthand and began to take pride in my notes, for it had a sort of an inspiraation about it, that enthused one to become a court reporter. The trial had been a very lengthy one, and there was several hours dictation, but I had resolved from the first, that if at all possible, I would take the entire trial and transcribe it. After considerable wrestling around for two or three weeks in company with one other fellow, we succeeded in accomplishing the feat, being the only ones out of the class of fifty or sixty. It made about sixty pages of closely written matter, and it was no small task for an amanuensis to perform. We were both very proud of our success, and fixed the transcripts up in fine style, and I still retain mine. The other fellow, who we will know by the name of Binns, was one of those peculiar characters we seldom meet. He had been a very adventuresome lad, having run away from home when young, and traveled all over the West and South, stating that at one time, after having been away from home for some time, and but a kid, he became financially stranded. He was going around in a very melancholy mood, when he happened to find a penny, with which he purchased a postal card, and wrote to his mother. Though his action in leaving home so young could but be condemned, yet his act in investing the one cent in the manner he did, is certainly commendable. After leaving school, his roving disposition again seized him, and, after reaching the Pacific coast in a box-car, succeeded in securing a position in Washington Territory, afterwards engaging in the fish and oyster business for himself, but finally again engaged in shorthand, and was following it the last I heard from him.

After taking the evidence which had been given in the murder trial, I got along very nicely with shorthand, and in fact most every way, only the outlook for a position was very discouraging, as some of them had already wended their way homeward, completely disgusted, never expecting to secure a place; and besides, my borrowing money was grinding on my conscience to an aggravating extent.

It had reached that point where it seemed like throwing good money after chances on bad, and to say that the future looked dark and gloomy, is placing it mildly. I did not want to leave school until I had something in view, neither did I want to continue to borrow money without any flattering prospects of being able to repay it. As would naturally be supposed, by this time I was becoming quite well acquainted with a large number of students, and was in a position to have considerable sport; was getting to be a fair foot-ball player, and learning to hold my own with things in general, but oh, that money business! something had to be done.

There were two large hotels in town, both of which did a good business. One of these, about three quarters of a mile from the school building, and in the central part of town, was in the habit of keeping one of the students from the college, as a general roustabout, for his board and room. One of the fellows who had been there, was going to leave, and he told me about it being a good place for a fellow whose currency was short. The very idea of my working for board while attending school! I could not at first consider it at all. I had been boarding at the college all the time, with ten of us at the table, five of each sex, and meal time was generally looked forward to with a view of having a sort of a young picnic; and then, the hotel was a great place for the boys to lounge around, and the thought of my meeting them there, was more than my pride would stand, so I did not take it. Another fellow got in there, but he only remained a week or two, during which time the prospects of my getting into anything that would enable me to earn any money by the use of my accomplishment, was growing darker and darker, daily. Driven, as it were, by a troubled conscience, more than absolute necessity, I went to the hotel. I didn't look forward with very much of a dread as to what the work would be there, but the thought of the students passing the hotel and see me at work, if they should, was anything but a pleasant thought. While it was no disgrace, nevertheless, I could not help but look upon it as such. The room they furnished me was comfortable, but not very large, and not so pleasantly located as it might have been, but as there are sometimes exceptions to rules, such it was in this case, for the people were very nice to me, and treated me as one of the family. I could not have asked for kinder treatment under the circumstances. My main duty was to rise about four o'clock in the morning and start two or three fires, thus allowing me to get my work done and everything ready before any of the students would be on the street, and the remainder of the time I would invest in my room.

There is not a more disagreeable feeling than to have one's pride crushed and being continually trampled under foot, and while I was not often seen by any of the fellows from the college, around the hotel, there would be times when circumstances would be such as to have me carrying a pail of coal as they passed. I could feel the blood rush to my face and the perspiration start afresh; then I would retire to my humble habitation, smooth out my troubled conscience a little, and go to school. While this may not seem very hard to some, it was more than I trust I shall ever have to do again. Not so much for the position as the circumstance. Had I been in a strange town, where I was a total stranger, it would not have hurt me in the least, but there is a peculiarity about everyone, and that was one of my peculiar characteristics. During this time I was learning rapidly, in more ways than one, and I improved every spare moment, hence was, as I thought, getting in pretty good shape for a position.

While I was at the hotel only about six weeks, I gained some very healthy and lasting experience, which I have not, as yet, forgotten. My brother in Butchertown finally advised me to come down there and try my luck, and after considering the matter for a time, and making the necessary arrangements, I decided to go.

There are few times in life more touching than leaving school, especially when a number of warm friends are to be left; however, it is something that one encounters in life. After having been accustomed to mingle with them daily, then to grasp their hands in farewell, when, beyond all probabilities, it is for the last time, it is no joke, by any means. But, of course such partings depend largely upon the depth of friendship with a person, and, with me it meant a great deal. However, circumstances were such it seemed wisdom to go, so after the usual hand-shaking on one fine May morning, I turned my back upon the old school ground and the town of Hardstudy, forever.

CHAPTER VIII.

Life, no doubt, should be a scene of happiness;
but, largely from our own fault, it is true, all
know that it abounds in many trying scenes. It
is somewhat pitiful to see the young and the gay
brought suddenly face to face with the stern realities
of life, and care and trouble and sorrow take up
their thenceforth unceasing abode with them; and
yet the only thing to do is to take up the burdens
of life with a brave heart. A prominent writer
expressed my sentiments when he said: "As life
advances, does it not often seem as a vessel going to
pieces; as if we were on the broken fragments of
a ship, or in a solitary skiff, on the waste of waters? Can we say there was ever a truer saying
uttered, than 'Human life is a subject which we
all delight to contemplate? It is, alas! to be
feared that few of us sum the matter up aright.'
We are constantly wishing every period of life at
an end. The minor longs to be of age; then to
be a man of business; then to make up an estate;
then to arrive at honor; then to retire; and death
soon closes the scene-shifting.

"Life has been compared to many things; often-est, perhaps, to a river, down which we voyage in a boat. At first, we glide down the narrow chan-nel, through the playful murmurings of the little brook, and the winding of grassy borders. The trees hang their blossoms over our young heads, the flowers on the brink seem to offer themselves to our young hands; we are happy in hope, and we grasp eagerly at the beauties around us; but the stream hurries on, and still our hands are empty. Our course in youth and manhood is along a wider and deeper flood, amid objects more striking and magnificent. We are animated at the moving pictures of enjoyment and industry passing around us; we are excited at some short-lived disappointment. The stream hurries us on, and our joys and our griefs are alike left behind us. We may be shipwrecked, we cannot be de-layed; whether rough or smooth, the river hastens to its home. At length, the roar of the ocean is in our ears, the tossing of the waves beneath our feet, the land lessens from our eyes, the floods are lifted around us, and of our further voyage no mortal knows. The wind is always off shore, and no boat ever returns."

Were I to sum up the course of life in a few words, I would say, "The course of life is a rug-ged diagonal between duty and desire." It is some-what pathetic, when we consider how completely the youthful dreams of life are often disappointed. It has been said, "A true man will lose on

time in getting down to earnest work in life," but
experience taught me, if a man do this, to be a true
man, he can never be a stenographer and a true man;
for, though he may be ever so willing, if he can't
get a "job," he can't get down to earnest business
without losing some time. It is true, we are not
to seek for some easy passage through life, for we
are liable to find that our paths will lie amid rocks
and crags, and not on lawns or among lilies;
over precipitous mountains, not along the pleasant banks of winding rivers. We have got to
take hold of the tough knots of life and try to
untie them. We would say, let every man be
occupied, and occupied in the highest employment of which his nature is capable. There is
one consolation in this action, that is, there will
always remain to such an one the inner conscien-
tiousness that he has done his best.

As the train pulled out of Hardstudy, I gave
one long look at the little town in the beautiful
valley, turned my face forward, and I was rush-
ing forth to meet the stern realities of life, as ignorant of what the future held in store for me, as it
was possible for one to be, and yet as full of ambition and anticipation as my limited imaginations
would permit. I did not anticipate all smooth
sailing, neither did I anticipate it would be quite
so rugged as it had been. I did not then so fully
appreciate the fact as I do now, that there is a
vast difference between a dollar earned and a dollar saved. I had figured largely on the income

tax, out gave little thought to the output. Who can think over his past life without wishing he might have one more trial, and that to start with the experience we now have? Oh, what a glorious success we would make of it, to be sure! But as it is, we can only profit by the experience of others. While my brother Harry had his business headquarters at Butchertown, he resided at Deadville, a little suburban town about ten miles away, he being on the road a great deal of the time; and, as accidents will happen, such we might consider it in this case, for after a ride of an hour or so, I came to a junction, where it was necessary to change cars, and who should be on the train I was to take for Deadville, but Harry! It had been several months since I had seen any of the folks, and under the circumstances which surrounded my life just at this time, it is needless to say I was "tickled to death" to see him. Seemed I never saw him look so good before, and knowing what he had already done for me, I naturally felt a little under obligations to him.

He took in my situation at a glance, and no doubt in sympathy with me, for he did everything he could to encourage me, and before night I thought half the battle of life was victoriously fought. There are times in life when kind words are almost as valuable as gold, and are something all can give if they will. Along in the afternoon we reached Deadville, and, to say the least, the name is very expressive. The buildings, some of

them at least, gave unmistakable evidence of having been built many long years ago, and some of
the inhabitants bore evidence of having lived in the
days when it was fashionable for the men to wear
long hair, and had forgotten to change their custom when the rest of the civilized world did; but,
regardless of the dilapidated, long-haired pedestrians that infested the place, there were some very
nice residences.

The backbone of the town was a large agricultural college, founded by some benevolent old
fellow when he joined the silent majority. At the
time we arrived there, I believe there were about
five hundred students in attendance, and to say
they were a mixed up lot of knowledge seekers,
is placing it in a very mild form. It was so
arranged, that any one with good intentions could
enter the school, even if he was completely financially stranded, and work half of the time and attend school the other half. Taking a retrospect-
ive view of the situation, I sized it up about this
way: The school was composed of the children of
wealthy people, who had become unmanageable in
the city and sent them there to get them out of the
way; this, however, composed a very small portion
of the school. Then there were a few that were real
anxious to gain an education, and who were not
able to obtain it in other colleges, but the larger
portion was made up of those who had made a
stab at life, and it had culminated in failure before they were more than twenty-five, and deciding

to take a moral, as well as a financial turn in life,
they had taken up a course in school, with a view
of making preachers or lawyers out of themselves.
While the farm in connection with the college
might have been large enough, everything went to
show that it was either not profitably cultivated,
or else the soil in° and around Deadville was of
the non-productive sort; as Wm. Nye puts it,
"Had to engage stone masons to plant their
corn." for they could not commence to raise
enouge to feed the hungry multitude, let alone
clothe them, hence they depended largely on
donations from the dying rich in the East, and
their expectations from this source were very
often gratified; but sometimes it would seem their
Eastern friends were not dying with the regularity
necessary to keep them in good shape.   One of
the most peculiar features of the students was
their dress.   Some large clothing house in the
East would have a large stock of clothing that had
gone out of date, misfits, etc., and after carrying
them in stock until tired of them, they would
donate them to the college, and from this dona-
tion the boys were clothed.   It was, first there first
served, hence the best pushers would get to the
pile first, and pick out their suit, which would be
of a respectable looking nature, but it was nothing strange to see some poor, meek looking chap
standing around, a few days after the distribution,
stove into a pair of pants six inches too short for
him, and a coat made after the Prince Albert

fashion, at least five years too old for him. One can better imagine than can pen describe, what sort of a spectacle two or three hundred boys dressed in this manner would present. The girls seemed to fare better in regard to the dress business, as they usually looked much more respectable; whether they were better served in the dress line, or whether they were more particular about their toilet, I am not prepared to say.

The course of study took seven years, and should have been quite thorough, but it would always seem sad to me to see them entering upon a seven year course of such a life as that when they were anywhere from twenty-five to forty years old; yet, with a great many of them, it seemed about the only avenue in life that was left for them to tread. There is no doubt but that if we could learn the secret life of the students in such a school as that, we would learn of some very sad disappointments and crushed hopes. With some of them, the countenance and looks gave unmistakable evidence of a troubled mind and a disappointed life.

The next morning, in company with Harry, I visited Butchertown, which was the first city experience that had ever crossed my path. The place then numbered about two hundred thousand people, and was to me a lively town. The first sight of it disgusted me, and it seemed utterly impossible that I could ever look upon such a place with any thought of calling it my home; in after years I looked back upon that thought and wondered, Could it be possible?

It was a very cloudy day, raining a little, and smoke thick and heavy, and everything so different from the surroundings at Hardstudy, my heart grew light and the thought rushed through my mind, This or farming. While I can now think of this and smile, it was to me then a very serious matter, for it did not seem that I could ever live there for love or money.

After taking in the town for an hour or two, we called upon a gentleman that had formerly been a great friend of the family, but was now engaged in business in the city. Harry informed him during the conversation which followed, that I was "looking for a job," and, while he was very courteous and expressed a willingness to do all he could for me, he was not in a position to do anything just then, as business was getting dull. He was trafficing in real estate, and real estate had taken a tumble. After both a pleasant and disappointed visit with him, and one other old time friend or two, we returned to Deadville and invested the remainder of the day very pleasantly.

Business called Harry out of town, and there was nothing for me to do but lay around or go back to the city and rustle for a place to earn bread. Mustering up all the courage I could command, I took the morning train for the city, and while I did not anticipate that the business men would run out into the streets and pull me in, in their bloodthirsty desire to secure a "competent stenographer" (which the letter in my pocket said I was), I did expect that some of the mighty financiers of that burg would give me a job. Not knowing what better to do, I went to the same place Harry and I had been the day before, to let them know I was still in the field of business, but, strange to say, they did not have a very long list of fellows looking for a man of my calibre. The sun coming out, and the smoke clearing away somewhat, I resolved to tackle every man or boy that I met, for something to do, until I got a place; that is, where I found them in an office. Some of the large business buildings I would canvass from cellar to garret, but in every place I met about the same response, if a response at all. Some places, where the offices would be peculiarly arranged, and being ignorant about everything, I remember on one occasion particularly, I went in and tackled the boss for a place, and got a negative reply, but as I was making a thorough canvass of the building, walked out, and walked into the next door and tackled the man sitting there, when I discovered the fact that the office had two doors, and he was the same man that had just told me no. I discovered the mistake about the time the salutation was completed, and whether by an act of providence or from my frightened looks, I am not prepared to say, but sufficeth to say, instead of kicking me out, as most men would have done under the circumstances, he only smiled, spoke pleasantly, as I receded through the door.

Another fellow told me he had placed an ad in the paper for a stenographer, and the next morning the hall, clear to the head of the elevator, was crowded full of applicants; it appeared, so he said, the town was full of them. This was indeed a flattering outlook for one in my position, and, after trying time and time again, I finally concluded he was about right. It really seemed to me there must have been an alarming influx of steno's from some source, or business was dreadfully dull.

Though I met scarcely nothing but disappointment all day, I was not as much discouraged that night as I was when I reached the city in the morning, for I had been partially initiated to city life, and the thought that there was a possibility of my living there, flitted across my mind.

When I reached Deadville that night, I was so worn out I could hardly walk; tramping and trembling all day, had proven about all I was prepared for; however, the plan of operation, on reaching the city next time, had been previously mapped out.

Persistent effort works wonders at times, and finally clews to openings began to show up; most of them, when traced down, proved to be without foundation, but when a fellow is going to a certain place to see about something he has heard of, he can get a business move-up, but when he is just meandering along, not knowing where he is going, everything becomes so monotonous, he moves as though he was going to his own funeral. Late in the afternoon, I learned of a stenogrpher having committed suicide in the office, and was informed that beyond a doubt there would be a vacancy there; so, learning the location of the place, resolved to go over there at once and get in my application before it was too late. After starting, the thought of going before the other fellow was buried, almost haunted me, but the little experience already had, tended to develop my courage into what might properly come under the term "gall;" so, proceeding forward, reached the office while the boss was at the funeral. Things did not look very encouraging around there, and I pondered in my mind whether the poor fellow had become disheartened with the surroundings, or whether he could not read his notes, but considered more favorably the latter, for I have since learned that such difficulties will cause a fellow to think seriously of so doing. The people in the office, no doubt, thought I was a little too premature, and gave me no encouragement whatever; in other words, discouraged all hopes of anything like a position. This discouraged me more than anything yet; what was the use; a fellow could not get around in time; if only a few more of them would commit suicide or die, and give some one else a chance; but it appeared they would not do it.

Business was apparently looming up a little in my line, that is, I was getting onto more clues every day, and it now became a case of chase down rumors, and while in nearly every instance I met nothing but sheer disappointment, there was that desperation in ambition to secure a place, that every spark of information regarding a vacancy was fanned into a flame, by my heated imagination and overdrawn anticipations. Some places they made good promises, probaly would be an opening after a time, and one day I struck a fellow who was sure of a place for me, but wanted five dollars to put me on. This was altogether out of the question, for, had it been a house and lot for five dollars, I could not have purchased it unless the means could have been borrowed. Finally he took my note, with the understanding it was to be held out of the first month's salary. This time I thought the matter was sealed and sure, the place being about a mile and a half from where I gathered the information. Money was too precious for me to waste it on car fare, and all my navigation was done strictly after the pedestrian order. The sun was fearfully hot, but it was like a boy going fishing, the trip down there did not bother at all, but oh, the trip coming back! They were not ready for a man yet, probably would be after awhile, could not tell how long. The same old racket. What was the use; the town full of fellows just like myself, looking for work, and besides, quite a number of ladies, and only one chance in a hundred should there be a vacancy.

My advice to any one starting out, would be, to hang on; the prospect can never be darker than was mine, but persistent effort sometimes wins, even when fate seems to be against us. Two weeks had been invested in trying for a place. All this time railroad fare to Deadville had been drawing terribly on my limited exchequer, and something must be done. I had called upon Harry so long for money, it seemed like it was getting to be an old story, and the line must be drawn. It now came a time when some definite action must be taken to relieve my distressed financial condition, whether in the line of short-hand or not. I had been offered a place in a retail dry goods store in Hardstudy, but at such a small salary it would but little more than keep up ex-penses; yet, considering the way circumstances had shaped themselves, I wished the opportunity had been taken.

CHAPTER IX.

FROM BAD TO WORSE—FINALLY DRIVEN TO THE WALL AND TRY THE BOOK BUSINESS.

After carefully scrutinizing the papers for a few days, I saw an ad, which read very flattering: "Young men wanted, to do collecting, office work," etc. There was a snap, which would be a good way to earn a little money and get on my feet while looking for a place as a stenographer. I went down to see the man, walked into his office, told my business, and was ushered into his private sanctum sanctorum. He was an oily tongued rascal, wore a silk hat, and if I ever meet him again, and recognize him, one of us will probably get hurt; but perhaps we shall never meet, (at least I hope not.)

He put up a regular land office talk, and before he was through, I imagined I could hear the shekels jingling down into my jeans; nothing to do but a little collecting, office work, and whatever there was to do; to start at ten dollars a week, with the understanding of an increase in salary shortly. This was Saturday, Monday morning I was to go to work.

·Now that a position had been secured, I little questioned but what the worst was over, but any-one with any experience in life might have known he was a bare-faced liar, and me a sucker. The remainder of the day was invested in pleasure; great big fat position waiting for me, I spent a quarter foolishly on the strength of it, in visiting a panorama of Gettysburg, which was a fraud.

I was in good spirits when reaching home, but was somewhat surprised at the doubtful look on Harry's face when I told him of my excellent luck in securing employment. He cross-questioned me pretty sharply as to what the work was, but I gave him the same song Mr. Oilytongue had given me, so he finally agreed to go down to the city with me Monday morning, help me to secure a boarding place, and get me started. Talk about blissful anticipations, but I basked in them, for the next day at least, to perfection. Being under the impression the position was a very important one, and one that demanded early and prompt attention, in order to be on hand promptly at seven, we took the four o'clock train that morn-ing. While Harry was very good to me all the way through, I can not help thinking he made a very poor selection when he secured my boarding house, not that it was unclean, but with such a heartless people, and a people that lived so much better and higher than my pocket-book would ad-mit of my living. He gave me some more money,

some advice about keeping a sharp look-out and
not get worked, etc., and then left, as business
called him hence.

On reaching the habitation of his royal highness, I discovered that a number of other fellows
had secured a snap (?) also, and were to commence
work that morning. There was quite a string of
us in the front office waiting our turn; one by one
they went through the door, from whence, to all
appearances, they never returned, each man seeming to take about ten or fifteen minutes, and then,
as I afterwards learned, they were letting them
out the back door. It all looked a little suspicious, but that great big, juicy ten dollars a week
covered all seeming defects to me, and I waited
patiently my turn, which turned up about eight
o'clock. The man with the silk hat on, that had
engaged my valuable services, sat at the desk,
and upon being ushered into his presence and
the door closed behind me, he politely informed
me what my first duties would be. All I would
have to do would be to just go out and sell a
few books, showing me the prospectus I was to
carry, explaining how easy it would be; tell the
people they only have to pay so much per week;
and, despite the fact that I was not only disappointed but utterly disgusted when I learned what
my duty was to be, before he got through talking,
I imagined it was not so bad after all, and believed I could make a success of it. He gave ex-
plicit instructions that I should not carry the book

where it would be visible, but must carry it under my coat until I could secure a sack of some kind to conceal it in. Of course he took some money as a deposit for the prospectus, and after thoroughly dressing me down, said I had better go to my room and study up all that day, and come up the next morning, or, if I so desired, go out and sell some books, and then come up and report. I attempted to adopt the latter "clause." He talked to me until I was under the impression it was, without question, the most wonderful publication that had ever been promulgated, and had no doubt but what a mere presentation of the wonderful work meant a sale. He was careful to inform me that, to make a success, I must be interested in the book myself, and that I must have faith in its value; but the bloody prevaricator, if that had been any indication, every man, woman and child I passed, would have purchased one, for he had puffed it up until I thought it really had no equal.

Imagine me, when upon reaching the street, in compliance with instructions, I placed the valuable volume under my coat, so people could not see it. The very idea of a large book like that, tucked up under the little summer coat, caused me to look like a snake after having swallowed a toad; but, believing that to be one of the secrets of success in the business, the poor book was scrunched up under that coat just as far as possible. I imagined every fellow I met, laughed at me, and no doubt but what most of them that saw my deformed looking condition, did.

Before going to the room, however, I went to the post-office, and upon inquiry, received a letter in answer to one of my applications for a place as steno. Without losing any time, I answered the call in person, found a vacancy; said he was much pleased with the neatness of my application, and that their head man was off for a few months and they would give me a trial. The fellow was just as pleasant as any one could ask, for a man in his position, but said he would like to try me before engaging me, as I was inexperienced. To this day I am unable to account for the miserable failure made, for he dictated slow, and while I had nothing but an old pen to write with, I should have gotten it. There was no question but what I was excited, and he knew it. I could not read the letter at all, and he, appreciating my embarrassment, said for me to go and study up that day, fix up for writing, and come down the next morning. The rest of the day was invested in rubbing up on shorthand, but I could not sleep good at all that night. Next morning, on reaching the place, the old fellow was as jovial as ever, but said, after considering the matter, he did not believe I would be able to hold the place, as it was a very difficult one, and it would hardly be possible for an inexperienced man to do the work; gave me considerable encouragement, saying that

I would be all right with a little more study, and to take some place not quite so hard as that one, to start with.

Notwithstanding the encouraging words the old fellow gave me, when leaving the place, I had the blues, and besides, it commenced to rain. There was nothing now but that book, on which to earn bread. I returned to the room, and studied until noon. By this time the rain had almost ceased, and about one o'clock in the afternoon I went out to "take some orders." Oh, that some one could have kicked me before I got out of the yard, taken the book away from me and saved me the bitter experience that followed. Such a dreary afternoon, and such a dismal task! I did not have sense enough to go out among the class of people that would entertain even a book agent with respect, but struck among the people who had servants to answer the ring of the door bell. House after house was visited, and I did not even get a chance to tell of my "wonderful treasure;" the door was either slammed in my face, or I was met with, "My mistress told me not to allow any more book agents about the place!" flung into my face as spiteful as could be. That kind of talk to a tenderfoot like I was, stuck too deep to be explained on paper. All the gall and courage formerly brought to my assistance, proved of no avail upon these occasions, but, true to the task, I kept pegging away nearly all the afternoon, and while it may seem strange, it is, nevertheless true, the only person that I could get to even listen to my wonderful story, was a poor, old, crippled-up shoe-maker, that could not have bought a book had he wanted to, and I doubt if he could have read it, had some one made him a present of it. I had tried so long to get a chance to tell my tale, then when I found a fellow that could not get away, and seemed to listen, even a little unwillingly, I talked an arm nearly off him. The man in the silk hat had told me not to take "no" for an answer, and while the poor old fellow kept per-sistently pleading and assuring me he could not possibly afford to buy, I kept hanging on, until, through actual shame I sneaked out.

Never in my existence thus far on earth, have I looked upon the gloomy side of life in such a manner; in other words, human existence never portrayed to me a darker picture, from my own stand-point, than did it that evening. I had in-herited a disposition that hated the word failure, but it now came to me with all its horror, for failure had been the result of my efforts, and a dis-mal failure at that. Only one man to listen, and he a crippled shoemaker; it looked to me like a pretty tough record, and does yet. It appeared the elements were in a mood somewhat similar to myself, for they began to pour fourth abundantly, and I and the book meandered back to the room more like a funeral procession than anything else.

There I was, completely disgusted with life, home-sick, life-sick, out of money, among strangers

and it raining like fury. All thought of investing
another night there, weighed down upon me like
a monster, and there was a feeling about my heart
that can not be explained. Some people may
think there is nothing in homesickness, but I pre-
fer to have the measles any time, in preference to
a real bad case of home-sickness.

There was one outlet. I had money enough to
take me to Deadville, but the thought of telling
Harry of my brilliant exploits as a business man and
representative of the monstrous book publishing
establishment of the East, weighed not a little
upon my mind. It was growing almost dark; the
rain was to me dreadfully dismal; the train would
leave for Deadville in a few minutes; the temptation was too great; I would chance meeting Harry,
tell him the truth and take the consequences, it
could be no worse than the book business. I
gave the folks of the house to understand that the
press of business called me out of the city in
haste, rushed to the depot, and was soon moving
for Deadville. I must admit I felt rather sneaking, as the train moved along and I pondered
over the brilliant career of the past few•days.
But the grand satisfaction of again reaching Harry's, it cannot be explained. After putting up a
pitiful talk that my best efforts had been exhausted, and proven futile, together with my dilapidated looks, won their sympathy and they did
not even reprimand me.

Supper over, matters commenced to loom up a little, and it once more began to dawn upon my somewhat bewildered mind that possibly life would be worth living sometime in the dim unborn future, and that it was best to not yet give up in despair.

A thorough canvass of the matter with Harry, brought us to the conclusion that my build was not particularly adapted to the life of one endeavoring to raise the standard of humanity by introducing world-startling productions of the pen, under the title of a book agent, and that my future success in life depended largely upon my dropping onto some other avocation for a means of earning bread.

Next morning, I returned to the city, for the purpose of continuing my search for a position as a rapid pen pusher and marvelous typewriter operator. The precipitation which grand old nature had been so extensively engaged in, the evening before, had ceased, but it was yet cloudy and dreary. The very sight of books made me turn sick at heart, and almost become disgusted with literature in every state and form.

About noon, an extraordinary and encouraging clue was discovered, which resulted in my securing a place as clerk, roustabout and stenographer combined, and about one p. m. I rolled up my sleeves. The long thought of and much anticipated fortune was certainly now within my grasp, or, at least, so I now imagined. There seems to have been no special agreement reached, as to the amount of compensation I was to receive for my valuable (?) services, but, full of ambition and self-confidence, the pen commenced to wield at my command.

It was a wholesale commission house, and business rushing and the place would have been difficult for an experienced man, hence it is easy to imagine the chance I stood. The head of the concern was a regular old crank, if there ever was one; he expected a fellow to wheel boxes, keep books, act as cashier, make out bills, and be a stenographer and typewriter all at once. By a desperate effort on my part, a fairly respectable showing was made that afternoon, but he did not have a typewriter; the letters, what few were written, had to be placed on paper by hand and pen. My penmanship did not abound in flourishes, nor,, we might add, in legibility; this, together with the hurry and excitement that surrounded me, caused the writing to look rather bad beyond a doubt.

Regardless of all this, my spirits that evening were far above par, and the thought of failure never once entered my brain. Next morning, I was on hand for duty early, and, after rustling around until nearly ten o'clock, the old man got hot, and fired me outright, and that without a very long or eloquent valedictory speech, either. His speech was very short, and might well be said to abound with needless adjectives. The only thing I don't now understand, is, why he did not bring his boots into play to impress upon my mind that the valuable services rendered by me were not at all satisfactory, and were no longer needed. With a sort of a horse thief look on me, I meekly inquired if he was not going to give me something for what I had done. In answer to this, he handed me a dollar, with, "It's more than you have earned."

There I was again! Such a recommendation to start out with to look for another job. I cannot say it was with any very flattering prospects before me that I meandered down the crowded street, of that apparently busy place, but, discouraging as it may appear, I was not so utterly disgusted as when retiring from actual service in the book venture.

Business in my line was undoubtedly getting better, for it was so I could get onto jobs, even though they proved too much for me. I rustled the remainder of that day with no avail. The time for which my board had been paid, had expired, the money Harry had given me was all gone, but a very small amount. There was nothing to do but go back to Deadville, which I did, told my tale of woe, and again won their sympathy.

As a last resort, I decided to rent a typewriter and go into business for myself. Once more Harry made me a loan, and by a stream of lucky moves, I found a place where a fellow was willing to give me office room with him, and do his work,

thus giving me a good place to make my headquarters. Eight dollars was what they charged
per month for the rent of the machine. The man
where I was to have my headquarters was very
nice and did all he could for me. While it may
seem strange, it is nevertheless true, after working
a day or two I became interested in soliciting
business, got out a lot of slips showing samples of
my work, also prices, and commenced to distribute
them around in various offices, putting up a good
talk wherever possible, and in a day or two prospects looked much brighter. Whether by chance
or an act of providence, I am unable to say,
a certain law firm needed some work done in my
line, and one of the fellows took a fancy to me,
presumably more through pity than otherwise, but
he was good and treated me white. He came over
and asked me if I could bring my typewriter and
do some work for them that afternoon. Of course
I went; he read to me, and at night I had earned
two dollars. I was the happiest man in town;
there was no question in my own mind now but
what the foundation for a successful future was
laid. Out of the money Harry had furnished
when starting up this new deal, I had purchased a
mileage book, which furnished means of transportation, and in case of emergency, I could go without dinner. I did not get the money that night,
but next day about noon I went around to see them.
At that time, I had just ten great big juicy cents
in my pocket, and besides, was actually hungry,

having been on my feet all the fore part of the day. After getting the two dollars, the first pass was to eat.

During my solicitations, I had struck quite a large job of work over across the river, and a few days afterwards, in going over to see about it, struck a permanent position, which was welcomed with open arms.

CHAPTER X.

Although Butchertown had experienced quite a
boom in real estate, I struck the town at the wrong
end of the boom; real estate men were pushing
hard to make both ends meet, and some of them
were failing even in this. Some men in good
localities were still hanging on, making a little
money dealing in suburban property; one of the
latter named was the place I secured for the season a permanent place to earn bread.

It was about the middle of June; everything
looked promising ahead. The agreement was, I
should receive forty dollars per month until the
first of September, then an increase in compensation would be taken into consideration. This
was highly satisfactory to me, there being but one
impending difficulty: I was to furnish the typewriter, which, of course, I was in a very poor
position to do. I could never stand to pay eight
dollars per month for one, and how on earth could
I attempt to purchase one. Was in debt then, as
far as I cared to go, but under the circumstances
there was nothing else to do. One hundred dol-

lars for the typewriter, to be paid in $25.00 in-
stallments, Harry agreeing to help me out when
needful, or rather when necessary, as it was needful then.   How I did squeeze that little forty dollars every month, but squeeze as I might, the
twenty-five dollars could not be stored away to
meet the notes that came due with such startling regularity.   All the time my account with
Harry was growing larger instead of getting less;
however, I was prospering very nicely with the
work.   The office was in what might have been
used for a store building, a long, narrow concern.
In the front was the real estate office, in the rear
an express office, the latter being in charge of a
young lady.   There was hardly work enough to
keep a fellow busy, but there were no other office
men at all, hence my work consisted of everything
from office boy to coachman and general manager
while Mr. Moneymaker was out, and he was out
most of the time.   The letters did not average
more than five or six a day; considerable writing
and copying to do, but nothing very difficult. The
first resolution passed in my mind was, I would
show Mr. Moneymaker that I was not afraid to
work, hence the office was swept out each morning and everything dusted off before he came
down.   No matter what there was to do, if it was
anything my ability was able to cope with, I acted.   Sometimes it was to go out and assist in
cleaning out some new houses just completed,
sweep out the loose shavings, anything to invest

the time in the best manner possible. Some days he would be away all day, then all there was to do was to play manager and talk with the express company's representative.

From a social standpoint, except in office hours, life was rather barren for me, home-sickness often visited my room, but it lacked the terrible pangs of disappointment that had accompanied it at the culmination of my book representative career. As time wore on, acquaintances began to be made at the boarding house, some of which I afterwards sorely repented; some, one especially, is a warm friend to this day. Another, my acquaintance with him, proved very expensive, as the currency he borrowed years ago for two weeks is still at large.

Early in the fall, I arranged to visit the people at home. Mother was anxious for me to come, and Jennie wrote awfully encouraging about my coming; so, one evening, finding Mr. Moneymaker in a very pleasant mood, the subject was broached and the request granted. Ten days off and a trip home. Only those who have been taken from quiet home life and thrown among strangers, can fully appreciate what those words mean, what a feeling they bring to a person. The thought of seeing all the old landmarks that have been watched from childhood, plenty of fresh air, nothing to do but enjoy life. Time could not pass fast enough between this and the time for starting.

After visiting the folks at home a short time, the country intervening between the old homestead and the ranch that had so often been visited by me in times passed, was crossed.   I was tolerably well pleased to see Jennie, and she was tickled to death to see me; in fact, she was so tickled, excited, or something, that before I could recover myself upon entering the door, she deliberately kissed me.   The thoughts that flitted across my mind were never reduced to words, the blood rushed to my face and perspiration started on my forehead, but presuming that that was the proper manner we must meet, said nothing, dropped into a chair and was soon waiting for the kids to retire. The ancient man was well supplied with haps and mishaps that had transpired during my absence, but owing to the heated condition of the elements, he retired rather early, as did the remainder of the family, and soon we were left alone.   She talked and talked, and so did I; patched up all the old "scraps" that had taken place before my leaving, all of which, as those who have had experience know, has a tendency to make one think he is sailing down life's river on flowery beds of ease.   After the clock had voiced its sentiments a few times, I and the faithful creature tied at the gate, wended our weary way across the country, and sweet sleep ended the scene.   During the visit, one other trip was made over there; possibly two; the last one was a regular heart-breaker, or should have been, at least.   Jennie acted as though

she thought more of me than she did of the brin-
dle cow, and I commenced to think that without
her, life for me would be but a life of snow-storms
and earthquakes; but time called me hence. The
worst feature of a visit with home folks now came,
the time when farewell must again be uttered.
While the thought of a visit at home is one very
pleasant to a boy, after having been away for a
year or two, the thought of returning to his place
of labor among strangers, saying farewell to
mother, while the tears are rolling down her cheeks,
little sister crying, and a very heavy feeling about
your own heart, it, to a very large degree, offsets
the pleasure experienced; yet, of such is human
life composed; we must taste the bitter to appreciate the sweet.

On the return trip, I stopped over one day at
Gentleburg and visited with Harry Jones. This
marked another oasis in the social world for me.
Harry was such a fine fellow and such a friend.
If the world was full of such young men, human
life would be lifted at least one degree higher, and
it would be well worth living.

Monday morning found me at the office. Mr.
Moneymaker had been quite busy, and had been
forced to secure the assistance of a lady during
my absence. Business did not boom any more,
but, on the contrary, gradually grew worse.

About this time the acquaintance of Billy Goodfellow was formed, and has continued to grow
ever since. Partially through his influence and

partially as a means of sociability and recreation, I was induced to unite with a detachment of some sort of a business of the State Militia. We drilled and drilled, and learned a little, but it was a tough gang, to say the least. We kept it up for a long time, then some big fellow, in name only, came down from the State Capitol and saw us drill, gave but little encouragement, and the company became disgusted, got into a little scrap, and disbanded. When they re-organized, I did not fall in line, although the second attempt made proved successful; but my ambition to be a soldier bold soon wore off.

Business continued to grow so much worse, Mr. Moneymaker said he could not afford to pay me the salary he was, much longer, and thought it best, for my own good, that I look out for another place, in the meantime he would assist me all he could. Under the circumstances, this was all that could be asked of him. He promised not to reduce the salary for a few weeks at any rate, and during that time every effort was to be made on my part to secure another place.

Most every Sunday was invested at Deadville, coming back to Butchertown in the evening. During the time of my probation, one Sunday evening as we were coming in from Deadville, I picked up a paper off the car floor, and about the first thing my eyes glanced across, was, "Stenographer wanted." The next morning at an early

hour my application was in the mail; it was one
of those initial addresses, and no idea could be
formed as to who it was.

Nothing was heard from it for two or three
days, when, on going to dinner one day, imagine
my surprise at finding a letter, in answer to my
application, from Messrs. Cleanmen & Co., one
of the largest packing establishments in the West.
They requested that I call at their place of business, which immediate arrangements were made
to do. That afternoon, Mr. Moneymaker did not
come in, so about 3 o'clock I went down to the
packing establishment, which was some two miles
away. Upon showing the letter, I was ushered
into a room where a keen eyed man took me in
tow. One would have thought by this time my
embarrassment would have worn off, when endeavoring to take dictation, but such was not the
case with me. A large cud of gum was being unmercifully crushed and re-crushed in my mouth
when the keen eyed man said, "Take a letter."
The system which I then wrote was one in which
lines played a very important part; he gave me a
yellow pad of paper, no lines on it at all, and instead of asking for some that was properly ruled,
made an attempt with what was given me. He
talked and I wrote at it, then retired to the typewriter room to transcribe. The gum was cut with
valor, sweat rolled off my forehead, and after a
struggle of about fifteen minutes, returned to the
keen eyed man with a sort of an apology for a

letter. There were two or three very bad breaks in the letter, but instead of pushing me out of the door, he took my application together with the letter just ground out, and told me to follow him, at the same time informing me that he was looking for a stenographer for the general superintendent's office.

We looked up the man wearing this title, who proved to be a fine fellow for a man in his position and build, the latter being of the corpulent variety. Few men who have and hold sway over from one thousand to fifteen hundred men all the time, can hardly be expected to wear a cheerful countenance twenty-four hours every day; hence we may reasonably expect to find a stern man, stern, but exceptionally good for a man in his position. The keen eyed man exhibited the letters; the application was fine, almost a perfect letter, the other one was bad. I offered the excuse that there were no lines on the paper; this, together with the anxious look on my face, seemed to strike Mr. Smith, the superintendent, in quite a favorable manner. He cross-questioned me for awhile, among other things telling me I would be expected to furnish my own machine, This, of course, I was fully prepared to do, as the machine was in good shape, and the use of it weighed lightly with me just then, when between me and a position. I did not desire a repetition of the book business, nor a long, fruitless search, as had been my former experience.

In a very short time he told me I could commence next day, at the price named in my letter, which was forty dollars per month. . Had I then really understood what a position with that firm meant, I would have accepted thirty rather than have missed it. The agreement was, I should go to work there the next day, so I returned to Mr. Moneymaker's, about as happy as a fellow could well be and live.

CHAPTER XI.

MYSTERIES AND MISERIES IN A MAMMOTH PACKING HOUSE.

Mr. Moneymaker was pleased to learn of my success, and arrangements were at once effected, whereby I should change places the next day. Inasmuch as he had been very kind to me, I did not feel that it would be justice to leave him without first getting his writing all done up in good condition, as he would not have the assistance of a stenographer thereafter, hence I worked for him until in the afternoon, when, taking typewriter in hand, I meandered out of the office and started for the new field.

Only then did I appreciate the kindness he had shown me. I could not expect such lenient treatment where my steps were now leading me, and, in fact, my first impression of the packing house had not been at all favorable. Everything looked like it was not a nice place for a fellow to stop, and then, the atmosphere was thick with a smell that it seemed one could never become accustomed to having it crowded up his nostrils all day. It was such a large place, so many men around, and everything taken into consideration, when com-

pared with the peaceful little office my lot had
heretofore been cast in, it was not at all an inviting place.

About four o'clock in the afternoon, I and the
typewriter put in our appearance where the keen
eyed man was, handed him a little note of excuse
from Mr. Moneymaker, for being so late, and we
were ushered out to what was called the "slaugh-
terhouse office," which was used as Mr. Smith's
headquarters. It was a terrible dark place, yet
clean. About six or eight men were working
in there, but the location was not of the best.
There was a large cooler on either side, and daylight gained an entrance from but one end, hence
it was necessary to use artificial light most all the
time; and, although it was on the third floor, it
was always a little damp, even in summer time.

When getting in there just at the close of the
day, things did not look particularly inviting, and
I really wished I had never come down at all; was
it possible one could live in such a place, all that
noise around there, the clanking of chains, moan-
ing of dying cattle, squealing of hogs as the life-
blood was oozing out, bleating of lambs, all this
coming up the stairway, sent the cold chills over
me, and once more, thoughts of the quiet, peaceful farm life flitted across my mind; but the die
was cast, and there was but one thing to do, that
was to push ahead.

There are many peculiarities about packing-
houses, that one, not familiar with their workings,

never dreams of. There are also many astonishing things connected with it that will interest a close observer as long as he may be connected with such an establishment. Such a place to study human nature, such a diversity of people working there, such a variety of machinery, and all these things taken together, interests one until he soon forgets his surroundings. One rarely ever tires of watching the cattle being driven in on one side, run into their little chute by themselves, from whence they never return alive; see them fell to the floor with one stroke of the mallet, then swung up, their throats cut, and before you can hardly realize it, the man called the "header," has taken the hide off the head, turned it back on the neck, and severed the head entirely from the body. The animal is now past danger, and it is pushed along down the endless chain that is constantly in motion. The blood where the cattle are being killed becomes very deep, and is run off into a gutter, caught in a basin below, and afterwards dried and used for a fertilizer. The heads are immediately picked up, and every particle of them utilized. This is one of the characteristics of a packing house, nothing is lost that can possibly be utilized in any way, shape or form.

After the cattle, have their heads taken off, they are thrown on the floor, partly skinned, then hung up again and the remainder of the skin taken off, then dressed and pushed around into the

cooler. All this moving is done by means of endless chains, consequently there are cattle moving
in every direction, on what is known as "killing
beds." At first, it always frightened me to go in
there, and it seemed impossible to cross the room
without being struck by some of the bleeding
creatures as they are being pushed back and
forth. This place, however, was one of Mr.
Smith's favorite resorts, and after having worked
there a few months, at one time I stood there
among the moving carcasses, with book in hand,
and took dictation from him.

We sometimes hear people, who have heard a
great deal about the packing business, tell about
pork packing, and how the hogs would come in
at one end alive, go out at the other, lard and
bacon; however, the struggle of "going through"
is more protracted and complicated than would at
first seem to the casual observer. It is true, they
may slaughter them with wonderful rapidity, yet
the curing of pork is a very particular business,
and is in itself a profession. The pig does not
allow his life to glide from him as does the cow or
sheep, but gives all within radius of his voice to
know that he is not at all pleased with being hung
up by the hind leg, and complains bitterly when
the knife is thrust into his heart. When we think
of one man standing all day long, continually
thrusting the sharp knife into the quivering hearts
of the poor fellows, is it any wonder he goes out
at night and gets a little drunk?

The most touching scenes around a place of this kind, is where the poor, innocent looking sheep and lambs are slaughtered. They lay down their lives so manfully, and rarely ever utter an audible complaint. The manner in which they are induced to the slaughter house, is unique. It is a well known fact that wherever one sheep goes the others will all follow, but it is often very difficult, and sometimes next to impossible, to get the first one started in the direction you want them to go, as they seem to cling together and huddle closer, instead of leading off as a bunch of cattle will. The plan used there, was to have an old sheep, familiar with all the hooks and crooks of the house, take him over to the stock yards, secure the bunch of sheep desired to be taken to the house, then turn the old sheep in with them. As soon as the gate is opened he starts back to the house, and, true to their natural inclinations, the rest follow. It is a very easy matter for the drovers to get them over to the house, and as soon as they are fully ushered in, the old sheep works his way out as quickly and quietly as possible and sneaks off, leaving the poor decoyed creatures to their inevitable fate. Soon he is hurried off for another bunch, and so he works, perhaps for years. I have sometimes thought if the animal creation really have a conscience, such a sheep must have troubled dreams some nights after having led his fellows to the slaughter all day long, taking into consideration they were "strangers in a strange land," and he, used to the ways of the city, especially after some days having led from one thousand to twelve hundred to their death.

The mode of slaughtering the innocent sheep, is at first sight, touching, to say the least. They have a low table, constructed with pegs about eighteen inches high, and five or six inches apart along one side. The sheep are laid on that table with their necks between the pegs and their feet on top of the sheep before them; after the table is full, the man that does the killing comes along with a knife, sticks it right through their neck, and then cuts out, thus severing the entire throat, then bends the head back, breaking the neck. It really seems too bad to slaughter them in this manner. They apparently offer no resistance at all, but meet their fate with, perhaps, a closing of the eyes, kicking a few times, and their spirit has taken its flight to a realm whence no man knoweth, while their body is on the road to mutton.

One gradually becomes hard-hearted as he lives around a packing-house; so many knives, men are daily getting hurt, chain falling on their head, knife slipping, or something happening to scar the poor fellows up.

There are some parts of the house where daylight never reaches, and it is very much like a coal mine in that respect, the large coolers, the freezers and places in the cellars. In some of those places, the frost never goes off the pipes, winter or summer, and the climate is in keeping with the pipes, hence great care must be exercised in the hot summer weather; this I learned by experience, which resulted in a large doctor bill.

It was so late the first afternoon when I got there, and Mr. Smith being out, he concluded to wait until the next day to commence on me. With this information I made my escape about six o'clock. The office hours commenced at 7 a. m., half an hour for dinner, and, as I afterwards learned, sometimes seemed there was no limit to the length of time one might be expected to work in the evening, before office hours were over. The seven o'clock business in the morning was a settled fact, half hour for dinner was all right, and if the work was done at half-past five, then it was time to quit; if not, when a fellow did get through office hours closed.

There was no suitable place to board near the packing house, and as I was somewhat acquainted in the vicinity where I had been stopping, I concluded I would remain there; but, in order for me to get down to that place by seven o'clock, it would be necessary for me to rise at an extremely early hour, as compared with the time I had been rising. Up to this time, half-past eight or nine o'clock had been office hours, and the office only two blocks from where I was living. Could it be arranged to go two miles and get there at seven?

The old lady who was "master of ceremonies" where my room was located, was quite good in some ways, but as cold and heartless as a person could well be in others. She was never sociable, and about all she cared for those stopping with her, was for the money she secured at the end of the month for the use of the room. Some time in the day, during my absence, she would arrange the room; other than that, one would hardly know there was such a person about the house. Every article of furniture had held its present place for years, judging from all appearances. It was useless to think of depending upon her to wake a fellow, so an alarm clock was the only hopes. This was secured and perched upon the table, but the rules were so strict about getting down on time, it kept me worrying all the time, and all hours of the night found me rolling out to see how long it would be before the alarm was going to perform, until, sometimes I would be so completely worn out by morning, it would voice its sentiments and never arouse me from my gentle slumbers at all; then, by some act of providence or otherwise, I would be awakened about half-past six: On such occasion, the near route would be taken, and this on foot. By going down a railroad track, crossing some yards and going along the river, the distance was very materially lessened. Two minutes for arranging wardrobe, and the soles of my shoes would commence to touch terra firma occasionally. After a time, custom caused me to awaken at a sufficiently early hour, and a great difficulty and trouble was overcome.

Mr. Smith proved to be so very kind to me, that the thought of never being able to become accustomed to packing house life, soon wore away, until it finally got to be that the only objection to be found was the extremely long hours.

Most of my dictation was taken after six o'clock at night, then allow the notes to remain over until next morning and transcribe them. His mail all being local, it would accumulate on his desk during the day; when he would reach the office about six he would commence to go over it and dictate to me as he read it, thus causing me to remain any length of time in order to complete the list. One other disagreeable feature was the Sunday work, for the Sabbath was very unbecomingly observed most of the time around the place. On Sunday morning we would not have to go down as early as on other mornings, and would perhaps quit a little earlier, nevertheless, we were supposed to be there.

In this place, most of my work was of a clerical nature, and an elegant opportunity was afforded for learning about every feature of the entire business, as my duties called me to all parts of the plant. It was really interesting to study the different mechanical arrangements, all in motion at various portions of the plant, all power being received from large engines, perhaps located a block or two away; then the ice machinery proved an interesting topic for study. Ice machines are becoming so common they are hardly classed with the curiosities any more.

In December of this same year, Harry and his family moved from Deadville to Butchertown, purchasing a nice place there, and I took up my abode with them. It is needless to say that such action met with my hearty approval, for it was far better than living among strangers. In order to reach the place where Harry lived, from the packing house, it was necessary to walk across about three quarters of a mile of very lonesome neighborhood. It was along the river bank all the way this distance, to the street car line leading out to Harry's, and the distance was dotted a portion of the way with some very suspicious looking shanties; the other portion of the way was along a railroad track, on rather high grade. In the fall and winter it was always dark when coming along here at night, and I invariably imagined some one was going to murder me for my money, or the money I would be supposed to have. After leaving the railroad track, there was only a path, the river on one side, the shanties on the other.

One terrible dark night, as I was going through a very lonesome place, there was a fellow in the path right ahead of me. His actions were very queer, and there was no question in my mind but what he had it in for me; just cut my throat, take my money and throw me into the river. How easily he could do it, nothing be left to tell the tale. Though the atmosphere was chilly, my body grew hot and cold, at brief intervals, my. head felt funny, and there was a very peculiar feeling about my heart. That he had a dark lantern, there could he no question in my mind, as was the conclusion formed, that he was there for no good purpose. When one's mind is concentrated on a certain thought, it is wonderful with what rapidity it can traverse a subject, and it is needless to say that all my imaginative powers were now operating on the subject in the path before me.   To turn and run; would be but to show that I was afraid of him; this would not be wise; to engage in a hand to hand conflict would not be wise either, unless the case demanded it, and I decided such would not be necessary unless I failed to retreat at a sufficient rate of speed to keep out of his clutches.

Having resolved itself into a case of where action was absolutely necessary, I made a desperate bound, keeping as close to the shanties as convenient, and I shot by him before he could have time to act, and to say that sand flew for the rest of the distance to the car station, is expressing it mildly, for I am yet confident the fellow was hanging around there for the sole purpose of getting gain in an unfair manner.

At another time, as I was meandering up the railroad track, after dark, though a clear night, yet not so desperately dark as on the evening above referred to, there was a very large dog concluded to give me a chase.   It has always been one of my failings to have a dreadful dislike for the dog species, and on this occasion my love for that portion of the quadruped family was not increased in the least.

He was barking quite loudly as he started from one of the colored shanties that stood off some distance from the track. He was several rods away when I first discovered he was coming directly at me. A small dinner basket was the only weapon at hand; there was no use to fight him, and being one of the number who believe it better to be a live coward than a dead hero, I at once headed down the track at the top of my speed. Mr. dog apparently increased his pace about this time also, and there we went. It seemed to me that at every bound about ten or fifteen ties were being passed, and the bounds were being duplicated in rapid succession, too. This was kept up for quite a distance, but, leap and bound as I might, the fact became apparent that he was a better turfman than I, for he was unquestionably gaining, and that rapidly. He had the steep embankment to climb, but it did not detain him but a very short time. We were both making excellent time, yet I soon discovered his was more excellent than mine. When it came to the point that my feet would not more than leave the tie until his would reach it, matters were entirely too uncomfortable for further procedure, and becoming convinced that ere long he would reach the tie before my hind leg had left it, I decided to turn and try to cause my uncomfortably close follower to think I was dangerous. Stopping suddenly, drawing the basket up as though death and destruction would descend with it, I brought it down directly in his face. It was so unexpected, he stopped, stepped back a little, and by my showing considerable more bravery than being actually possessed of, I succeeded in persuading him to abandon the chase. Such occurrences as these did not, as you may presume, tend to make it a pleasant walk by any means.

In this manner I worked for some fourteen months, not, however, without an increase in compensation. The lessons learned were of fully as much value to me as was the currency received, yet both were accepted gracefully. At the end of fourteen months something occurred that caused me to think I would be able to forsake shorthand altogether.

CHAPTER XII.

In the office which I have before described, the business pertaining to sales in a certain portion of the city was handled, cash received, account sales made up and turned in each day. After I had been in the office a little over a year, this position was vacant and tendered to me, and as it paid more than I was getting, besides, being of a more elevated character, or at least appeared so to me, I took it. It was not an easy task, but rather one that required very close attention; however, the promotion caused me to feel like one of the firm, hence, could do about anything.

About this time we received word from a lady friend up in the country, that she and her boy would come through our town on a certain date, en route for a distant land to visit a relative. Her experience in traveling had been very limited, and of course if we could meet her at the depot, it would be nice. She was a very nice lady, and we would be glad to see her.

Just as my luck usually was on such occasions, Harry was out of town on the eve of her expected arrival, so my lot was to meet our expected guest at the train. While, as already stated, she was a very nice lady, she was extremely corpulent, weighing in the vicinity of three hundred avoirdupois, and never having traveled a great deal, she did not take into consideration what trouble a cart load of baskets, grips, etc., all filled with articles of a various nature, would cause in changing cars in a city.

· The train was late; after ten o'clock when she arrived; the boy was of course asleep. One glance told the story. She had luggage enough to swamp a man, the kid as limber as a rag and as heavy as a piece of lead. After some scuffling around, visitor and her luggage were unloaded. I grappled the boy under one arm, clutched what luggage I could manage under the other, and took up the march. Visitor carried the remainder of the moveables. Poor woman, she imagined that every bell that rang in the vicinity of the depot was ringing for her to get off the track, until it seemed there was no place on top of the face of the earth for her. It was necessary that all my persuasive powers be brought to bear to convince her that her time had not yet come to cross over into eternity, but to get a move up and let's be going. After worrying street-car conductors, surprising the natives, and encountering a few other difficulties, we succeeded in reaching the point of compass for which we were steering.

Prosperity seemed to be my lot for a short time, and everything passed along smoothly. My experience in handling cash had been so extremely limited, that sometimes it proved embarrassing to have a pile of money poured out upon the desk, and one night when balancing the cash, it would not balance. There was no use to figure, something was wrong. Next morning I tried it again, but try as I might, there was a shortage in the cash. What a mean feeling it did cause; not so much for the loss of the money, although I was in no position to lose that amount, yet the thought of not being able to account for it, hurt worse. The cash was never all deposited in the bank at one time, so the shortage could have been carried for months, as we were never checked up very closely, yet the terrible uncomfortable feeling made life perfectly miserable for me. I did not mention it for some time; finally, when Saturday night came, I resolved to break the news to Mr. Smith, let come what might. The only explanation that could be given, was, that in making change, or counting a large pile of small money, gold pieces had been allowed to pass for something else. This explanation was offered; Mr. Smith looked at me in a manner he had never looked before; yet, even while under the stern gaze of his keen eye, there was even a more comfortable feeling than I had experienced for several days before. There was the sense of having done the right thing, regardless of what might follow.

He did not say much, and there was really no telling what to expect on my part. The next pay day I took from my pay enough to make up the deficit. Shortly afterwards, Mr. Smith came in and threw down some money on the desk, and in a quiet tone told me to take out enough from that to make up the shortage; this, he was doing out of his own pocket. The satisfaction with which I informed him that the shortage had already been supplied from my own pocket, can better be imagined than described. He gave me another keen look, though more pleasant than before, yet said nothing of importance, and matters went along as of yore. This lasted for two or three weeks, perhaps a little longer, until one evening Mr. Smith sent for me to come into his private room.

These packers had branch houses in most every large town in the United States, or at least a great many of the Eastern towns, and some in the West. Mr. Smith advised me that they were having some trouble with the house at Gentleburg, and asked how I would like to go up there. It was the very place I had often wished to live; but the question was, would my limited experience enable me to do the work. He informed me that the manager of the branch houses had enquired of him for a man, and that he had recommended me. After studying a short time, I asked to have until the next day to decide, to which he of course agreed. After consulting Harry that night, it was decided it would be best for me to try it, so the next morning I went to the office with that intention. Upon investigation, not altogether due to inquisitiveness on my part either, I learned that there seemed to be a leak in cash matters at Gentleburg, and the manager had enquired of the superintendent for a man that could be trusted. Mr. Smith gave me a very favorable recommendation, saying, that whatever I said could be banked upon, and that there would be no question as to my word. Of course this was all brought about, or largely so, at least, by my shortage in the money drawer and the disposition made of it.

Arrangements were made for my departure for Gentleburg, which was to take place the following Saturday. You will bear in mind that this is the place where Oscar Jones lives, and there was no time lost in advising him of the new change. He was of course pleased to know that I was coming there to live, and so planned that my stopping place should be with him, as his people lived there now. With the prospects ahead of me, the old ambition of growing rich breaking forth anew, the excitement of leaving, and all, seemed to overcome all thoughts of being homesick at the thought of leaving Harry. There was a sense of relief in the assurance of not having to report to that old slaughter-house office every morning at seven o'clock, month after month, and work from ten to fourteen hours each day.

Sunday night, my back was turned upon Butchertown, and after a few hours' ride was at Gentleburg. The circumstances in connection with the house there, were not as favorable as my anticipations had led me to expect, yet it was more pleasant, in many ways, than where my lot had been cast. There was more fresh air, shorter hours, and more liberties; besides, my duties did not keep me in the office all the time.

The office was located in a very lonesome part of the town, especially after dark, when the wholesale houses were closed. The general surroundings were not inviting, from the fact that one of the men was discharged outright the morning I went there, and I took his place. This would naturally cause the other fellows to look upon me in rather an unpleasant way. The manager of the house there, more as a matter of policy than anything else, treated me very nicely for a short time. At that time I did not surmise there was any policy about it for him, but, having had enough said to me that I might know how I stood with the house at Butchertown, and the ones who held power and sway, there was little use of trembling from fear of anything except unfair play. If their policy game did not work, that they might resort to this, was something that was not so pleasant to brood over.

The accounts were in a dreadful shape, every stub had been torn from the check book, and balances forced just to suit the occasion. Entire charge of the accounts was at once turned over to me, which did not at all meet the approval of Mr. Brown, manager of the Gentleburg house.

My home being with Oscar while at Gentleburg, I formed the acquaintance of one Timothy Slocum, who was also a stenographer, and who has played a very important part in my life ever since. He was a stenographer for a railroad company at the time, a fine fellow and one who was quite congenial to me, hence .we soon became very warm friends. He, together with Oscar, caused life to be very pleasant in a social way, besides, they had a number of friends there with whom I soon became acquainted.

Things at the office did not go at all smooth; the beef kept shrinking, car fares ran beyond all reason, Mr. Brown was cranky because the cash was being checked up too close, and it appeared everything worked together for the common evil. When out collecting, they would arrange to reach the office about 6:30, so as to be sure and keep me there until seven, settling up. Finally, the fatal day came for Mr. Brown. In his turning over the cash, he reported an unreasonable shortage at a certain place, which of course to him I did not question, but the next day made a personal investigation, and discovered that he was simply making a steal. . This was immediately reported to the house at Butchertown, although Mr. Brown did not learn of it.

After this, quite frequently occurrences of like nature came up, in which circumstances spoke

too plainly to be mistaken, and of which a record was kept on the quiet. Among the other con-
tingencies of our force at Gentleburg there was a
large, tall fellow who went by the name of "Joe."
He had been a second class prize fighter, something
of a base-ball sport, but had proven only a partial success at either of them, yet as a beef handler
he was a success in every particular. To handle a
quarter of beef with him was a very easy matter. His past record was of a very gloomy character, and he would sometimes tell me stories of
his cut-throat experiences that would cause the
cold chills to run over me when we would be in
the office alone, late at night; in short, I was afraid
of him. Owing to some act which he had committed in the very recent past he was forced to
abandon his position and soon left the town. He
was a wonderful character, and although what
most people would term "tough," there was an
inner nature to his being, though seldom brought
to the surface, which was admirable. One of his
noble traits was to eulogize his mother.

Things went on with Mr. Brown at the head of
the concern, until early in February, when matters
came to a focus. Mr. Brown was advised that
his services were no longer needed, and a new
man placed in his stead. · It was a case of "from
bad to worse," as far as the Gentleburg house
was concerned. The new man had been with
the firm for a number of years, and had, as
far as they knew, been all right, but the tempta-

tion proved too much for him, and he fell back
into the rut he had escaped for years, that of partaking excessively of intoxicants.   For a time he
did splendidly, and after everything was running
in good order, I went back to Butchertown.   That
the new man partook freely of intoxicating bev-
erages I was aware, but had no idea [of what it
would soon lead to.

It was not at all pleasant for me to leave the acquaintances formed in Gentleburg; for even though
there but a few months, a number of friends were
left behind, when returning to Butchertown.   The
thought of again facing the packing house did not
loom up before my eyes with any great degree of
pleasure.   The purpose for which I was sent to
Gentleburg had been accomplished and of course
my return followed.   However, after my departure from there, the new man became such a frequenter of places where the flowing bowl was wont
to hold forth, that he soon lost his place.   On
one occasion he was on a protracted over-in-
dulgence in the beverage and continued so all
day.   He locked up the office, and would not let
people in.   When called up by telephone, he
answered that he was on a drunk, and not doing
any business that day.   This proved fatal to him.

For nearly two weeks, after returning to the
packing house, my occupation consisted of about
anything and everything that came along; at the
expiration of that time there was a position vacant in
the general office of the firm, which was secured for

me. Thus my intimate relationship with the packing house ceased, but as the office was only half
a block from the slaughtering department, my
situation was close enough yet. However, the
hours were not so long, and the office was much
more pleasant. My duties were, part of them, rather
unique. Part was in the stenographic line, only
a small portion of it, however, the rest of the
time being clerical duties and coding messages.
They used the wire extensively with their branch
houses in different parts of the United States, and
all the messages sent to them were sent in coded
words. This might seem to one to be rather a
small task, but when taken into consideration that
sometimes as high as fifty car loads of meat left
the house daily, and a list of the contents of each
car was sent over the wire to its destination, it
will dawn upon the mind that more of a task was
involved than would seem to the casual thinker.
For instance, a car of fresh meat was billed to
New York; the car contained so many cattle, hogs
and sheep. There were words in the book that
stood for most any number of each class of animals; cattle, sheep and hogs all on one page, in
different columns, but one line of figures designat-
ing the number of animals. By gliding down
the columns it was an exceedingly easy matter to
get into the hog column when you wanted to be
in the sheep column. When a branch house in
the East would receive the wire giving the contents of the car, they would sell from the wire, to

arrive on such a date. One evening, soon after commencing this kind of work, my eyes wandered into the wrong column, and instead of telling the car contained one hundred head of dressed sheep I used the word to signify one hundred head of dressed hogs. The hogs were sold, but when the car arrived it contained sheep. When the news reached the place, I presumed there would be nothing to do now but to look for another place, but it appeared they expected a new man on the job to make a few errors, and I was amply gratifying their expectations in this regard. After that, greater care was exercised on my part, and although followed for nearly a year, nothing of a similar nature occurred; but to say that such a position is a pleasant one, we could not. The chances for errors are entirely too great, and it necessitates one being constantly on his guard.

After returning to Butchertown my stopping place was with Harry, as before, and the trips across the vacant space between the packing house and the cars had to be spanned twice daily. There was a friend who lived up in our part of the town, and quite frequently we would cross this space together in the morning as we were going to the house. One morning, he went to cross the railroad track in front of an approaching engine, but missed his calculations and was instantly killed. He had but recently joined the benedicts, and was, from his own story, enjoying life in a sublime manner. He was a very faithful fellow, and

had been with the firm for years, but his occupation was changed very abruptly, and without much
previous consultation. The thought flashed across
my mind at the time, how strange it was that
learned men of our land should puzzle their entire
lives and endeavor to fathom the mysteries of the
future state, yet this man learned more in two
minutes than did they in a life time. His information was of course of no value to us, and we
did not care to follow his example to become edi-·
fied in this particular line at the present time.

All this time matters in a social line were almost
at a stand-still with me, time being so occupied
with other matters. After the intimate relationship that had in years passed existed between Jennie and myself had died out, like most young fellows, I lost confidence in the gentler sex, and did
not lose any sleep over them. Leisure hours were
either invested with Billy Goodfellow or in reading. While this sort of life may suit some, it,
after a time became rather monotonous to me; yet
all this time my social qualities were being cooped
up but to burst forth in terror in the near future.

During the year after having left Gentleburg,
Timothy Slocum became disengaged with the
railroad company that he had been laboring with,
and after rustling the typewriter in a wholesale
house for a month or two, secured another position with a railroad company which landed him
in the little town of Jolleyville, located a long
ways south of Gentleburg, and also south of

Butchertown. He had a very favorable position, but things were so different, and among strangers, that he was dreadfully lonesome.

There had always been a way back inclination about me that suggested the railroad business would suit me far better than anything else, although no definite plan of action had ever been mapped out as to how the change was to be brought about. The place now occupied by me was very good, and everything passing along smoothly; the code words became familiar, and often whole messages could be written without referring to the book, yet every sentence be in code.

In the fall of that year, Timothy wrote me there would be an opening in the office where he was working, and asked if I wanted it. It was real tempting, but the compensation offered was such a slight increase over what I was then getting, it did not seem wise to accept, and so the offer was declined. This created a spirit of partial dissatisfaction about packing house work which never left me. A few months later, another opening was reported by Timothy, which paid something more than the other one, and considerable more than the position where I was, so, after due consideration and figuring both pro and con, I decided to take it. The opening would occur the first of the year, and all arrangements were made accordingly.

CHAPTER XIII.

LIFE IN A NEW FIELD—RAILROADING—THE REAL
TERRORS OF BEING UNABLE TO READ
YOUR OWN NOTES.

It was on a cold Sunday night, January 3d, that a south-bound train from Butchertown bore what was left of my somewhat demoralized and bewildered frame. Little did I dream what the then immediate future held in store for me. Had such information been in my possession, no doubt the trip would never have been taken, but Monday morning would have witnessed my form at the packing house again. There is no doubt but what it is often far better for us that we have never been endowed with the faculty of solving the mysteries of the future, for, to some of us such knowledge would prove a curse rather than a blessing. While it may be wise to be always prepared for an emergency, there would be no joy in life could we always know of the trouble that would cross our pathway at various future dates. It is human nature to be hoping and planning for the best, and even though we may be bitterly disappointed in some cherished anticipation, nevertheless we have had some enjoyment which neither principalities nor powers can rend from us, in the now disappointed hope.

As the train whirled along that night, the thoughts of being severed from acquaintances and friends, also losing the home which had been afforded me with Harry, weighed not a little upon my mind; but the thought of living in a small town, together with railroad work, was a sort of balm for my wounds. Besides this, there would be the association of Timothy; all these things being considered, the thoughts of the future were pictured in rather more glowing colors before me, than they otherwise would have been. There was one thing about it that every person should take into consideration when making a change in occupation of this kind, and that is, we are changing a certainty for an uncertainty, and unless the circumstances are much in favor of the change, great precaution should be exercised. I have often wondered at the itinerant disposition of many stenographers, and my advice would be to stick to a good place when you get it, and don't think every other fellow in the country has a snap but you.

There was one other fellow from Gentleburg, by the name of Sam Perfumery, with whom I was slightly acquainted, working for this same company with Timothy; with these two we could doubtless pass our leisure hours profitably and pleasantly.

On reaching Jolleyville, both Timothy and Sam met me at the depot. This town was fine, about ten thousand population, and beautifully located on a rolling prairie. The streets and yards were all set with trees, and while everything was of course barren now, one could not help but see it must be very beautiful in the summer.

The boys were both stopping at the hotel, and, as would naturally follow, my name was placed on the register at the same place. So far, everything had passed along very nicely, but now the time had come. Up to this time my stenographic life had consisted in a very few letters each day, and never had I held a place where all the work was stenographic and typewriting; but now a new era was to open up. With the exception of what experience one could get in the traffic department of a large firm, I was ignorant concerning railroading, further than that I had seen trains skim across the country and traveled a little on them, walked on the track and rode a railroad tricycle, as explained in previous chapters.

It had been hinted to me that the chief clerk in the office where I was to earn bread by the sweat of my brow, was pretty rapid and hard to take, but I was chucked brim full of confidence, and thought none of them too swift for me. To hold the place, I found it would be necessary to write from one hundred to one hundred and twen- five letters each day; this, when compared with the fifteen or twenty that had been my number of

letters daily, looked extremely large, yet anticipation, backed up by confidence, acted as an impetus to keep up my courage.

I was taken to the office in the morning and
introduced to the typewriter that would be the
means of my making a livelihood. It was a
dreadful old affair; looked as if it might have been
used by Noah's private secretary. Then followed
an introduction to the fellows who were to be my
dictators, three in number, and every one with
a pile of mail a foot high. One fellow commenced
to dictate to me as soon as I got settled down,
and it appeared he would never get through; there
was one redeeming feature about him, however,
and that was, he did not talk very fast, and was
just as good to a stenographer as circumstances
would permit. After filling the note book about
half full of notes, he finished up his desk for the
day and the typewriter at once engaged my attention. It had been worn so long, and so loose, it
was like an old sawmill with all the wheels loose,
and when scrambling over the keys it made a sort
of rattling noise instead of a clicking sound, as
typewriters are wont to do. The rest of the day
was invested on those letters, as well as that evening, but before sleeping the book was clear.
There were so many phrases that were entirely
foreign to my limited vocabulary, hence I often
experienced difficulty in reading the notes. Next
morning, man number two tackled me; he was
not quite so bad as the first, was very easy to take,

and I got along splendidly; but, woe, woe, the
chief clerk had not as yet dictated to me at all.
Timothy had been doing the necessary work for
him until I could get a foot hold.

The chief clerk was such a frightful looking fellow, and apparently always mad, that I was afraid
of him even when he was not dictating, and it
seemed to be, as I have since learned, one of his
peculiar characteristics to kill a new man on the
start, if at all possible, and especially was it so with
stenographers. That he had it in for me, soon
became apparent, yet I anticipated no serious
difficulty in taking his dictation. Finally the other
two men were in shape, my book clear, and a
large pile of mail on the desk of the chief clerk.
It was now or never. All at once the silent monot-
ony was broken by "Get yer book," spoken so
quick and sharp that my poor heart was in my
throat already. The requested book was flopped
into position as gracefully as possible under the
circumstances, and pencil in hand, we started. We
started together, but it is needless to say we
did not end together. He commenced spitting
out the words at the rate of about two hundred a minute, and by the time one document
had been finished there was another one in the
works, and he all the time talking, as if he
would like to chew up stenographer, typewriter,
desk and all. I was just a "jumping and grabbing," as the saying goes, "here a line and there
a line," but still he went; finally he distanced me

entirely, and, during one of the brief interims
while he was catching his breath, I managed to
swallow my heart and gasp out something about,
if his time was not too valuable we could get
along better by not becoming so hasty in our
trip. The exact words used can never be re-
called, but sufficeth to say it only brought forth
some swearing at me, and I was there and
then given to understand he was not to be in-
terrupted in his dictation. With this brief rest
(?) we started again, and away we went like
unto the first time. The sweat was rolling down
my forehead; the pencil was getting dull, and the
note book was but one conglomeration of scratches,
dots, dashes and scrawls. Pretty soon he had
said all he wanted to about the mail, and I had
a few clews of what remarks he had made, but
was so completely tired out when the chase was
over, that it seemed I could never read them, and
there was no use to try. He had dictated some
messages alone in the mail that he wanted right
away, threw the stuff over on my table, turned his
back and acted as though his time was worth four
hundred dollars per minute. The cold consolation received when venturing something about the
speed at which we were making letters, gave me
to understand that there was no use questioning
any, but to go to work and write them off, or
throw up the job, that's all there was to be done.
Some·of the letters I could not tell where they
commenced or where they ended; some, I could

not tell who they were to, and then, tangled up
with all that muss there were some wires to be
written "right away." There was one thing certain, that "right away" business must be an in-
definite time, for, to get them off with any degree
of alacrity, was entirely out of the question. Oh,
those lucid anticipations and fostered confidence,
where, oh, where are they now! I almost wished
that there had been a millstone tied about my
neck and I had been cast in the deep in my
youth.

After a severe struggle, which lasted for quite a
length of time, a little batch of battered up,
scrawny messages were put on the desk of his royal
highness. I felt as though I would like to crawl
under the typewriter until he looked over them,
for fear he would commit some desperate depreda-
tion, or kill me with a paper-weight. I do not believe the fellow had a single ounce of sympathy
at the time; or my looks would certainly have
moved him to extend a little courtesy and leniency
toward me, but he did not; he seemed to think I
should learn it all in a day, take dictation just as
fast as he could possibly talk, and then transcribe
them instantly without an error, have them look
nice enough to frame, even if written on a typewriter that a professional could not turn out a de-
cent letter on.

Much to my surprise he did not kick very hard
about the telegrams, scratched a few of them, and
by writing them over, they went. That night

Timothy went back to the office with me, and, as
we both pretended to write the same system, or,
in other words, I attempted to write the same system that he did, he could assist me very materially in transcribing my notes. The trouble was,
there was so much of it that was not there to transcribe, and, then so many scrawls that did not look
like anything in the heavens above or the earth
below. Once in awhile we would strike something we could read, then we would read the correspondence all through and endeavor to fit a
sentence around the word. If the word proved
to be a root word to a sentence, we would be all
right; but, if it chanced to be the word "it" or
"is," that we could decipher, it will at once dawn
upon the mind of a stenographer that it would be
no small task to fill in the missing links. We
worked until nearly twelve o'clock; worn out and
weary, we went to the room. How I did wish I
might have the place I left at Butchertown back
again. It was only now that I realized what a
fine place that was. Before going home, however,
we had made a bluff at all of them. There was
but one hope that I would not be let out at once,
and that was, Timothy stood in pretty well, and
stenographers were scarce in that part of the
country. That the letters were nothing near
right, I well knew, but they were the very best
that could be done.

The next morning all went as smoothly as usual
until he came to look over the letters, and then

his cup of indignation "runneth over." For a time it appeared that I would not only lose my job, but have to flee from the wrath to come. His wrath finally subsided slightly, and he committed no rash violence, but used the pen freely in the body of the letters. A great many of them were re-written, some scratched up and allowed to go through, and some dictated over. But what was the use to try; should I ever be able to take his letters; how could a fellow ever have anything like enjoyment in life under these conditions.

After this, for two or three days he kept giving his letters to Timothy, and would rarely ever notice me except occasionally when something would go wrong he would turn around and cuss me a little. There was one fault he had, from his own standpoint, and that was, he was cross and cussed so much that it failed to have the desired effect when the occasion demanded it, as one would become accustomed to it.

Timothy was a congenial companion, and, together with Sam, we would invest what little leisure time we had. This time was very limited, however, as we worked about eighteen hours some days, about fourteen on an average, Sunday excepted.

After three or four days from the first escapade, Mr. Chief Clerk thought he would give me another chase, so, after remarkably brief preliminaries, we started again, this time, at about the same rate as before, but having been cautioned by Tim-

othy to brace up, and not be afraid of him, I succeeded in getting most of the addresses so he
could tell what they stood for, and an occasional
sentence. What a case it was of seeing the ter-
ribleness of man's inhumanity to man. He was
but working on a salary as myself; true, he was
getting more, but, nevertheless, I was an American citizen, just as much as he was, and to think
I must be treated in that manner, went very much
against the grain. Some people, in fact a great
many of them, seem to think a stenographer is
but one degree above a machine, and sometimes
they talk to their stenographer as though he was
hardly equal to the typewriter he operated. Such
treatment is not justice, and it seems to me if men
could but appreciate that their stenographer is
a human being, they would treat him with more
courtesy. Were I in a position to put in a plea
for the stenographic force of our land, it would
be on this line. As a rule, they are fairly well paid,
and usually do not have to work as hard as an ordinary clerk, but it is a lamentable fact that they
are not treated from a social standpoint as they
should be. We believe that any conscientious
stenographer will do more for his employer's interests, if treated as an employee, or treated as
kindly as are the other employees, than if he is
used as a dog. He is presumed to know everything, take all the kicks that float, and besides,
keep his mouth closed outside of office hours, of
anything pertaining to the business. If a stenographer does not try, then there is cause for finding fault; but when he is doing his very best, he
should have a little leniency shown.

CHAPTER XIV.

STENOGRAPHER'S LIFE FROM A SOCIAL STANDPOINT.

If there is any department of clerical work where exercise is needed, it is in the stenographic. To sit and pick away at the typewriter all day, hammering those glass keys, becomes exceedingly monotonous. For two or three months after reaching Jolleyville, Timothy, Sam and I formed about the extent of our associations, none of us being inclined to lead what, in modern times, is termed a sporting life, hence we were, to a degree, congenial.

When the weather permitted, as a means of exercise, we would roam over the prairie for a mile or two, feasting our eyes upon the beautiful scenery, which consisted in an occasional mole hill, or, a little stream with all the fish hooked out. Another favorite sport was, boxing; in this, Timothy wore the medal; I wore the large blue places on my arms and chest.

Sam had a peculiar failing for the gentler sex, and we had not been there but a short time until he was under the impression that at least half of the native girls of the town thought he was next door to perfection. He usually dressed as though he had picked himself out of a bandbox just prior to leaving the house; low-cut vest, white tie and a large (imitation) diamond stud in front; some-times, on rare occasions, a silk hat covered his head. Observing from his actions, and his talk, we learned that he was very much impressed with a certain young lady whom he had seen at a public gathering, and we resolved to have him the main performer in a practical joke.

It was the custom in that town for about half of the citizens to go to the post-office near six o'clock in the evening, to look at their boxes, or worry the post-master by asking for a letter which they had no hope or real expectation of getting. The young ladies of the town took a very active part in this part of the program. Our plan was, to write Sam a letter in a fine hand, describe how she would be dressed, and sign a ficticious name, advising him that she would meet him at the post-office, about six p. m., on a certain date.

About six p. m., on the date mentioned in the letter, Timothy and I walked around by the post-office, and who should we see standing there but Sam, dressed in his best, and sizing up, from head to foot, every person that entered the office. We quizzed him with all sorts of questions, and kept him in such a state of excitement that I doubt if he would have known his mother, had she passed in. Soon, he began to wear an uneasy look, and kept growing more and more impatient; such a state of affairs existed until about seven o'clock, when he gave up in despair and went home. This was huge fun for us, but for poor Sam, judging from the disgusted look which the back of his neck wore as he meandered down the street, it was far from being a pleasant evening.

While Timothy was a fine fellow, he had some failings which occasionally got him into trouble; one was, he would never arise in the morning until the extreme eleventh hour. Our place of sleeping was located about five blocks from the hotel where we were boarding, four blocks of the distance being on the principal street of the town. One cold morning, Timothy delayed action in arising until after I had been out for some time; finally, realizing that it had reached the point where it was a case of necessity, he arose, arranged his wardrobe hastily, or pretended to at least, and rushed down the street at no slow pace. To the pedestrians who were on the street it was rather a unique sight, for in his haste he had forgotten to fasten but one of those articles used to keep the trousers from falling off, commonly calles suspenders. This poor suspender was forgotten entirely, and was now hanging head downward, below his coat. One can well imagine the sight it presented as he moved rapidly down the street, and he did not discover the mistake until after he had marched into the hotel and was informed by one of the porters that some of his wearing paraphernalia needed adjustment.

After we had inhabited the place for two or three months, our acquaintances began to grow, and early in the Spring we attended a little social gathering, where we met a number of new faces, some of which attracted more or less attention from us; one of them, in particular, attracted more than usual observation from me, as will be seen later on. Miss Missionary, for as such we call her, was somewhat out of the ordinary in looks, and, as experience taught me afterwards, in actions; her education had never been neglected, however, having been educated in a private school; morally, she was almost perfection; but the secret of it was, she was the pet of the family.

Timothy had a fashion of sitting around the room, in the evening, with a sort of a far away, melancholy look about his face, that caused me to think he was allowing his mind to meander over by-gone days, or else he was thinking of some one left behind in Gentleburg. My persisting quizzing failed to bring forth any particular light on the subject, yet my suspicions were aroused to such an extent that I began to fear I would be left a widower in a short time, and through a friend in Gentleburg, I gained such information that enabled me to corner Timothy and force him to confess. It was like a thunder shock to me when he informed me he was to join the benedicts in the coming June. This information was imparted to me in April, and it was not received with any degree of pleasure. My association had thus far been almost wholly with

Timothy, and from a social standpoint the outlook would not, from the then present appearance,
be very flattering. There were two months left
yet, and I resolved to make the best of that time,
and did.

Among other things in which he was careless,
was the handling of money. At times, every cent
he had in his pocket would be piled upon the table and allowed to remain there until morning.
Repeatedly cautioning him proved to be fruitless,
so I resolved to avail myself of the first opportunity to teach him a lesson. One day, after receiving our pay at the office, about the middle of
the afternoon, I went into the room where he was,
and while talking to him, observed that his pay
check for the month was hanging on a small bill-
hook on the wall. It certainly was a very careless way of handling such documents, yet there
was no special danger. On mentioning the fact
to him it only brought forth a laugh on his part,
which but acted as an impetus to push me on in
my scheme. In about half an hour I again visited the room, and the check was still hanging
there. I went around behind him, and was talking about something on the desk before him,
which of course attracted his eyes in that direction. I was then standing between him and the
check, which enabled me to easily slip it off the
hook and drop it on the floor, and with one foot
push it under the desk. Then, in a jovial manner, I went around to the other side of the desk

and sat down, all the time keeping up a conversation, and at the same time keeping my foot at
work until the coveted document was entirely on
my side of the desk, when, stooping over, I picked
it up and slipped it into my pocket. At this time
I had no intention of allowing the matter to grow
as serious as it afterwards did. He forgot all
about his check until after he had taken supper
and retired to the room, then the thought came to
him with vengeance. He did not say anything,
but looked like a convicted train robber, and in a
mild sort of way, said he guessed he would go
down to the office a little while. It dawned upon
me at once that he had remembered the check,
but the matter had gone so far there could be no
harm in allowing it to go a little further, so I
allowed him to go without giving him any satisfaction. He went to the office, and just as he
was going into the room where he worked, he met
one of the boys, of not a very excellent character, coming out of the room. Imagination caused
him to think the fellow looked sneaking and
guilty. I went down another street, and after
waiting for some minutes, started over to the office
just in time to see him coming out, in somewhat
of a rage. He explained about the check, without hesitation, and of course I was perfectly
astonished. He then related about meeting the
fellow with a sneaking look, and was quite posi-
tive that fellow had the check. After some persuasion, I prevailed upon him to return to the

office with me, and we would take another look. We did so, and every scrap of paper, book, and everything else in the office was turned over from one to four times, but the search was in vain. The blood in Timothy's veins now began to become a little tropical, and nothing short of a round-up with the fellow he had met coming from the office, would be any balm for his wounds.

The large stores in town had a custom of allowing any one to purchase a small bill of goods, and in payment allow them to present their check and have it cashed. In this way, there was a slight danger of the finder getting money on Timothy's check, but the chances were only one in a hundred. My argument was, however, to try and convince him that any of the stores in town would cash it on presentation, if properly endorsed, and that this fellow could sell it to some bum, and allow the bum to cash it and leave town. He finally believed this to be about straight, and marched directly to the hotel to lay the guilty man out. The fellow he was after was playing billiards at the time, and Timothy watched him for some time with an eagle eye; and while to him he looked actually guilty, what could he do and how could he prove it. He watched him for half an hour; then decided there was no use, and we started back to the room. We had only gone a block or two, when the thought of advertising it in the morning paper dawned upon him, and was so firmly fixed, he would not give it up. It was now about ten o'clock, and he had been kept in this worried condition for about two hours, which should have been enough to satisfy me, but it did not. Every effort on my part was exhausted trying to get him to give up the idea of mentioning the theft to the newspaper men, but he would advertise it or die on the spot, so there was nothing to do but to tell him. It would never do to have it advertised; this was going too far, so I told him. To say that he was mad, offers but a poor explanation of his condition; he was going to completely obliterate me off the face of the earth at once, without further preliminaries, but the street was broad, and I took advantage of that. I did not get close to him until after he was asleep, and the next morning he was all right, only one thing, and that was, that I did not give it away among the boys at the office, which promise was made and afterwards kept.

He was like most other fellows when pierced by cupid's dart, he was boyish, and would go to Gentleburg at every opportunity. Although the space intervening was over two hundred miles, he did not appear to mind the distance at all. One week before the occurrence which inaugurated him as a benedict took place, he went up there and remained two days, and while there, as a sort of a foretaste of what was to follow, he procured the license, and came back with an importont air, carrying the precious document. He placed it in the archives of his trunk and allowed it to rest there during the day, but would feast his wistful eyes on the same in the evening.   When the week was up, he was very much excited, and in his rush to get started, took only what he thought of first.   After he had been gone a few hours, I received a message from him, stating that he had forgotten that all-important document, and for me to bring it up, as I was intending to go to Gentleburg the next day.   The poor fellow was worried over the matter, for he did not know whether he could secure another one or not, and, as we may well suppose, it would place him in rather an uneasy and awkward position.   Despite all these inconvenient and unpleasant experiences, he seems to be just as careless about such matters as ever.

He was gone for ten days, and after my return from Gentleburg everything looked as if there had been a funeral at the room.   It was so lonesome I could not remain there alone evenings, and invested a greater portion of the time at the office.

In the early part of June, there was a lawn tennis club organized in Jolleyville, to consist of twenty members, and, as good fortune would have it, I was invited to be one of the twenty.   The invitation was accepted with open arms, and this afterwards proved to be the nucleus for many pleasant hours.   The club was to consist of ten gentlemen and ten ladies, its object being for pleasure more than becoming experts at the game, and this being the object, it was a flattering success.   It worked something after this fashion: The club met every night about six, and would play until about eight, sometimes a little later, in other words, just as long as the balls could be seen. Then a general conversation would follow for a few minutes, sometimes longer, but in nine cases out of every ten, the conversation would last until it would be too dark for the gentler portion of the race to seek their several places of abode unescorted. Of course there was no harm in walking down the street about the same time some of the lady players did, and at the same time act as their "protector." It would take only a few minutes; but, then, when arriving at the gate, just over on the inside would be a very inviting looking hammock, or a large arm chair, the dog chained in his kennel and the old gentleman asleep. Where is the young man with his mind in its normal condition that would whirl on his heel at the gate in the very jaws of such an opportunity? Not here, I assure you, and the consequence was, it would be nine or ten o'clock, and often later, before my humble habitation would be graced with my presence.

It is one of the peculiarities of human nature, that anything we are successful at, in any kind of sport, or, we might say avocation of life, we take a delight in it; thus it was with tennis. While I never hoped to become an expert, I could hold my own and could do somewhat better than the average in the club. My zeal for the game has

never relaxed very materially either, yet the want
of opportunities for playing has caused it to wear
off some.

During all this time I had not forgotten Miss
Missionary, and while I endeavored to persuade
myself into believing differently, the fact was
nevertheless apparent that her appearance on the
grounds always caused a queer sensation to come
over me.   That part of my anatomy which pushes
the blood around, commonly termed heart, would
perform its functions with a more vicious move-
ment, and somehow everything seemed to go along
better when she was there.   If actions are any indication of matters of this kind, she did her part
to help the case along somewhat, too.

Her papa was of the antediluvian type, rather
queer, and as cranky as a crocodile.   There was
one redeeming feature which was largely in my
favor, however, that was, he was quite old and
sickly, and generally retired early or sought the
quietude of his room and would not put in his appearance any more for the evening.   Their lawn
was so inviting, it would make a pedestrian's
mouth water when weary, and on reaching the
gate, it took very little solicitation on the part of
Miss Missionary to induce me to haul my little
feet inside.   I have heard it said that a very good
plan is first to win the affections of the dog, next
the old gentleman and lady, and then the coast is
clear.   Experience afterwards taught me it was the
only way to attack that family, but I thought life

was too short, and as long as the dog was chained and the old gentleman remained under cover, I did not worry about which way the wind blew.

Competition is the life of trade, to be sure, but in some cases too much competition works hardships. In the commercial world competition has become almost a necessity, and is doubtless one of the saving features of the human family. It is the strict competition in the boarding house business that enables the poor stenographer to rush out at noon and get his lunch for twenty cents; fifteen, if times are hard, and ten towards the latter end of the month when he receives his salary in monthly installments; but, as stated above, there is competition that unquestionably does more harm than good.

About the time I commenced to think the girl and the front yard and the hammock and the arm chair were something entirely out of the ordinary, there was another fellow formed the same opinion of the same outfit. Of all the miserable, complicated, disgusting, competitions on the face of the earth, such as this, is the worst. It makes a fellow wish he might have ceased to exist in his youth, and to keep up with the procession and look finer than that other whelp, he will shine his shoes twice a day, shave three or four times a week and change shirts just as often as he can afford it. Then he has got to take her to everything that comes along, for if he don't, the other fellow will, and ice cream entertainments, picnics,

circuses, shows, theatres, livery bill and everything in this line has to go.   My brother steno,
let me drop you a little advice: When you get in
this kind of a fix don't try to buy yourself out; I
tried that; consequently, other fellows got all the
money I hammered glass for.   Mr. Spectacles (as
that was the name of my competitor in this trans-
action) never seemed to have very good sense
(perhaps he thought the same of me), but, nevertheless, he kept grasping every opportunity, which
was only semi-occasionally, as he valued money
more than did I.   Another place where he always
wore the winning badge, and that was, he was a
member of "our Sunday school" which I was not.

There was a member of the tennis club who,
on account of his peculiar stature, was known as
"Shorty."   His hair was just about as red as it is
possible for hair to be, and he was as comical as
he was little.   During the summer the burglars became very numerous in Jolleyville, and it was almost a nightly occurrence for some of the villagers
to have their houses plundered.   It happened also
that Shorty was a stenographer, which caused me
to have a friendly feeling toward him.

One eventful evening, the house where Shorty
stopped was entered and many articles of his
wearing apparel was confiscated by the klepno-
manial abstraction.   Among other things was a
pair of socks.   As would naturally follow, the
club sympathized with him, and in a quiet manner a subscription paper was circulated with the

express purpose of buying a pair of socks. The subscription was quite liberal, and an elegant pair of the nether garment was purchased, but the color was loud and flashy. A special meeting of the club was called, and after dispensing with necessary business, a presentation speech was made, in which Shorty was presented with the half-hose, in behalf of the society. This was the first knowledge he had of anything of the kind being on foot, and he drew up until he looked like but a kid.

Shorty was a first-class stenographer, and one of the many feats he performed, acting in that capacity was to read the notes of Mr. Jones, one of his dictators. Mr. Jones had formerly been a stenographer and they both wrote the same system. Mr. J. would sometimes take work to his home and would write the letters out in shorthand and the 'next morning Shorty would transcribe the notes without difficulty. This was somewhat marvelous to me, as it was all that I could do to read my own notes, and that when they were fresh and juicy; after they were a little cold and congealed it was extremely uphill work, and after real cold, an impossibility

By the middle of Summer, the work had become so familiar to me, and my dictators were not quite so rapid, or so I thought, at least, and the miserable sieges that had been experienced by me in the beginning now became more easy, and sometimes two or three weeks would pass without any serious trouble, then the one who had given

me so much trouble all along, the chief clerk,
would be angry when he commenced to dictate,
and trouble would invariably follow, and does to
this day, for it is an impossibility for me to cope
with the circumstances on such occasions.

CHAPTER XV.

CIRCUMSTANCES SUCH, A HEALTHY REALIZATION
FOLLOWS THAT A STENOGRAPHER
IS NOT A MACHINE.

Timothy's joining the benedicts broke the bands that had bound him, Sam and me together, and from that time we gradually drifted apart in a social way. Sam fell in with a very nice family, took up his abode there, and afterwards married the fair damsel of the place. Whether he was fortunate or not, time alone will answer. In his estimation he had captured a prize, as most people imagine they have when first married, but in many cases the gold soon wears off.

Soon after Timothy left me, I changed my place of abode, and fell in with a very nice looking young man from the East. Here, I tried my hand as a reformationist. This young man had been well raised, and from his appearance and manners it was evident he came from a good family, but, like many other boys, he had been spoiled entirely. He was a first-class man at his business, shoe salesman, and had few equals; but he had no more judgment with money than a child; besides this, he was inclined to sport, keep late hours,

and became altogether disgusting ere I was through
with him. He would receive letters from his
mother requesting him to be a good boy, and
then he would turn over a new leaf and come
home, may be for one evening, early, possibly
two, then it would all wear off. When leaving
the house, he always looked as if he might be
going out to have a picture taken. For several
months my efforts at reformation went on, until
finally I had to slip him out of town on a midnight train in order to keep his creditors off of
him. He was in debt on every corner; drug men,
hotel men, shoe men, dry goods men, tailors, and
even whiskey men mourned his departure. The
fact was, the longer I worked with him it seemed
the tougher he got, and it was a relief to get him
off my hands, for at the rate I was reforming
him, I was afraid he would soon become a des-
perado. He secured a place a few hundred miles
further west, and last heard from him, he was
doing well, or at least so the story went.

 · Early in the fall of this year, I formed the acquaintance of Mr. Vermont, another gentleman
from the East, who was principal of the high
school in Jolleyville. Afterwards our associations
grew to be very intimate. As there was a vacancy
in the tennis club, he was chosen to fill said place.

Mr. Vermont was of very light complexion, and
in female attire, with a wig, would have passed
very nicely for a lady, had it not been for a few
straggling, red, fuzzy hairs on his upper lip. His

education was quite complete, and fully covered his defects in looks, and he performed his duties as principal in a very credible manner. He had a failing for the opposite sex which hindered his progress somewhat, as his first assistant was a lady, and remarks were soon afloat in the school that he was using entirely too much time in consultation with his first assistant. Such matters are always largely overdrawn, but that this was bad enough, there is no question. He was always a warm friend to me, and it was anything but pleasant to have to part with him about a year later, when he returned to the East. His welcome letters are regular visitors, however.

All through the Summer and early Fall, few days passed that I did not see Miss Missionary, and all the time, that which the most learned of our land have never been able to explain, was slowly but surely closing its icy grasp upon me. There was a sense of satisfaction in going down the street about the same time she did, that could never be explained by me. That lawn seemed finer and more pleasant than any in town; in short, our acquaintance was ripening fully as rapidly as it does in most cases of a similar character, and all are, perhaps, aware of how rapid that is.

All this time, however, there was a cloud rising in the background that I was entirely ignorant of; the old man's anger was ripening about two paces to our acquaintanceship's one. I thought it strange that he was never around any more, but went blindly on, regardless of the approaching storm. Mr. Spectacles was the Reverend's right hand man and a regular wheel horse in "our Sunday school," and was continually entwining laurels around the old gentleman's affections and the piece of meat in his breast where most men have a heart. I don't think the old fellow had any heart at all; if he had, it had long since become ossified. The house was of a very ancient style and had probably stood on its present foundation for twenty years at least; the furniture was rich, but very old-fashioned, as was also the pictures that graced the walls; but here the heartless individual invested his time brooding over thoughts of, I don't know what. I am convinced of one fact, however, that when our humble frame flitted across his musty thoughts, anything but a pleasant sensation crept over him. Despite the old gentleman's efforts, the fact was evident that slowly but surely I was gaining ground on Mr. Spectacles, my visits were much more frequent than his, and on the more particular occasions when anything special came to town, I always called on Miss Missionary. "What fools we mortals be." All those hard earned dollars and shining quarters went like they were to be picked from trees.

. It is said that the rising generation may profit by the experiences of others, and thus save them from falling into many pits their fathers have worried through, but this is one of the pathways of life that nearly every man wanders through, re-

gardless of the advice he may have received or
may receive at the time.

Timothy and his wife, by accident took up their
abode just across the street from Miss Missionary's, and the first opportunity possible was em-
braced by me in having them become acquainted.
She seemed to like to visit at Timothy's, and so
did I, consequently we reaped much pleasant re-
venge on the old gentleman, to my ignorance,
however, as I was not yet aware of the brewing
trouble or approaching catastrophe.

In the Fall, the work at the office was so under
control that it rarely ever required my presence at
night, and from two to four nights in the week
found me at the wonderful mansion. The fre-
quency of the visits was partially brought about
by the desire for her company, and partly to be
sure Mr. Spectacles was not there. Of course
every time I would go, he would be wrathy, and
when he would go, vice versa. How strange it
was; the town was brim full of the fair sex, and
yet when one of us went with Miss Missionary to
some public gathering, the other one always went
alone; this, however, very rarely happened, as we
generally ascertained beforehand, and the other
fellow would ostensibly be sick on that occasion,
or be too busy to go, when in reality he would be
at home, prancing up and down the room, doing
something else besides singing Sunday school
songs; or, at least, my part of it was performed
that way, and, from the disgusted look he

would have on his face when we would accident-
ally meet on the street, I am confident his was
the same.   One night, we were at a little gathering, when he wished to speak to me privately.   We
went out into the yard and dropped into the hammock together.   He introduced the rivalry subject without any very fancy preliminary remarks,
and we were both stubborn and contrary.   An
aggravated coal or railway strike would have been
easily brought to a reconciliation when compared
with that conversation.   He said he had been in
a number of similar circumstances before, and
had 'always come out ahead, and I said I had,
too.   But both could make such statements with
ill grace, or we would not be wanting another girl
now.   I knew I was lying, and am pretty sure he
was, but, as all is fair in charity and war, I guess
there was no harm done.   We remained there in
the hammock as long as it was either pleasant or
safe, and then went back to the house, each with
his mind made up to come out victorious, or die
in the struggle.

Talk about competition! If such competition is
not a curse to mankind, I don't know where you
will find it.   About this time, the Americanism in
me had arisen to such a point that, when we
reached home, I told her I had concluded to with-
draw from the race, and perhaps would go on
farther west and invest the remainder of my miserable life in abstracting the life-giving blood of
Indians and wild animals, in chasing the buffalo,

etc.; got a little romantic, as it were. She cried, and I went home with the understanding that a final decision was to be reached a few evenings afterwards, when I was to call. What an example of "men are but boys grown tall." I was frightened to death, for fear she would take me at my word and allow me to go, and could hardly await the appointed meeting. The trouble was patched up very nicely, and it was several weeks before the matter was brought to a focus; however, one evening the affair culminated rather abruptly. I presume she had been reading considerable romance, and was under the impression that the only proper way to wind up such a case, was for her to faint, and she commenced to perform in that manner. The circumstances were anything but pleasant, for to have called the folks and have the old man come in, would have been worse than meeting a cyclone on the prairie; but, as romance always runs, she regained her consciousness in about the right time, and we patched things up a little, with the understanding that I was to call again as soon as convenient, to further the patching. Before that evening arrived, the old gentleman drew the line, and I was forbid placing my tiny feet on his sod henceforth.

If there is ever a time when a stenographer comes to the conclusion that he is something more than a machine, it is in a case of this kind. If he has any feeling at all, it is sure to make itself manifest under these surroundings. There was nothing to do but treat the old gentleman with silent contempt, whip Mr. Spectacles and tell the girl good bye. The first was easily performed, but the second and third were different; the second I did not wish to do, and the third I did not propose to do. One thing was certain, until the quarantine was lifted, my feet could never tread the sacred soil of his lawn any more, and an attempt at such, would have perhaps culminated in my having to scale the fence with a dog of the abbreviated appendage immediately in the rear, or have taken up my exit at the business end of a shotgun, neither of which I felt inclined to do.

After doing some tall, masterly thinking, I wrote Miss Missionary a letter that would have touched the heart of the sturdy oak, and directed it more particularly to the old gentleman, who must be respected by me under the laws of courtesy to the aged. After this, I turned my back upon the whole affair, resolved never to cross the threshold of any other female as long as I lived, rustled up some of the boys and organized a bachelor's club and resolved to so live and die. The rules of the club were strict; no one was allowed to walk down the street with a young lady without the 'permission of the president in writing, and three visits to any one young lady in a week, even by consent of the president, the guilty party was to give an itemized account of their conversation. Our resolutions were good and deep founded, but as brittle as an egg shell. Hardly a week had rolled away when I received a very courteous invitation from Miss Missionary, to call on her, stating the coast was clear, and that peace would reign supreme.

How she ever managed to curb the old gentleman's temper, I have never been able to learn, but it is needless to say that the invitation was answered without the least degree of reluctance. There was, however, a very heavy shadow of doubt in my mind as to what it all meant. Was it possible that the ossified piece of meat in the antique gentleman's breast had softened towards me, or was it a means of decoy to get me over there, and then have him pour out his wrath upon me? Thought kept suggesting the latter, but under the circumstances a fellow could almost have faced the king of the lower regions rather than have given up in despair.

I went, and the means used by her to pave the way for my visit, is as much of a mystery to me to-day as it was then, as he never spoke to me again except in a case of emergency, and then his words were spit out in such a manner as to cause the cold chills to creep over me.

Often and often have I looked for a small boy to kick me for ever accepting that invitation, but, under the somewhat romantic circumstances, and the blissful anticipation of bothering old Specks a little more, it seemed neither the earth below nor the heavens above lent assistance sufficient to keep me from yielding to the temptation.

I gave the bachelor club the slip the evening when accepting the, what then appeared the very gracious invitation. They never learned but what I was at home on that date, and every precaution on my part was taken to keep them in such blissful ignorance. The boys were very unruly, and it kept court in session most every evening, for a time, at least, until they became reconciled to their fate, then we got down to business, reorganized a German class, and before Spring we were pretty fair Dutchmen. During this time, the permit business was often outrageously abused.

The ladies becoming acquainted with the nature of our club, decided to organize one of their own, which they did, and instead of our accomplishing the purpose for which we were organized, it worked right the reverse. The joint sessions of the club were very frequent, and banquets given periodically. At the close of the year, we gave them a very unique banquet, which proved somewhat interesting, and for a time entertaining. Our invitations read, "Light refreshments served by our own skilled hands." On the evening of the festive occasion oysters were cooked, in order to have the room highly flavored, and candles were so promiscuous that the room was so light it dazzled the eye; when in full blast, the ladies were escorted to the dining-room. The refreshments were extremely meagre, but the numerous candles caused what little there was, to be fully up to the expectations, light.

In a short time, the ladies gave a banquet which so discounted ours, that we quit the business; and, to make a bad matter worse, a union of the clubs was formed. The rest of the story need not be told; the object of the formation of the club was most unmercifully trampled under foot.

Sam took an extended trip when he was first married, and while he was away my poor machine ground out his allotment of letters. My office hours during his absence were almost without beginning or end; about eighteen per day. It was at this time I made my highest record on the typewriter, writing one hundred and ninety letters between times of sleeping. They were of a good, fair average, but the mill had my undivided attention the entire time except while endeavoring to allow the other fellows' thoughts drip off the end of my pen onto the paper in hieroglyphics, which afterwards I was presumed to transcribe, and which really I did, partially so. On one occasion I wrote one hundred and ninety letters between times of sleeping, that is, between 8:30 a. m. and 11:59½ p. m. I was so miserably weary that evening that glory had no temptation or inducement in store for me, or I should certainly have written the other ten. It was a pity I did not, but when the girl said, after having walked all day, "she would not take another step to see into heaven," so I felt that night; I would not write another letter for love or money; but, of course, if the right kind of one, or large enough amount of the other, had been at stake, perhaps I might have worried through with a few more.

All through the early Fall, after the old gentleman lifted the quarantine, my graceful form wended its way to that beautiful yard, and after the evenings became too cool to occupy the hammock, we sat and gazed into the parlor grate, where the bright fire sparkled, all the time cupid getting in his deadly work on me, and at the same time the master of ceremonies of the lower regions getting in his work on the antique gentleman. The Fall days wore into winter, and on the cold winter evenings, with my body wrapped in a heavy overcoat, my tracks left their imprint on the beautiful snow as they bore me toward the attractive habitation. What did it all mean? What could it mean? We had both positively agreed we were nothing but friends; but, ah, my stenographic brethren, beware! the mysteries of human nature are deep and extremely phenomenal. It is like taking the first drink; you drift down the pleasant pathway, and before you realize you have made a mis-step, or that you are on the wrong road, you are on a precipice from which it is hard to escape.

The old gentleman was rarely ever mentioned, and when he was, it was usually brought about by me, and it never failed to bring forth such a peculiar look from her, that for fear of something terrible happening, the subject would be immediately diverted to more pleasant themes. I began to think, what kind of a fellow is he; my acquaintance with him had been extremely limited; all I ever knew him to do, was to kick and go to church. When on the streets, he always looked as though he had no friends on earth, and few on the other side, and that he hated all humanity, including his dog. This, I might add, was the appearance from a distance, as my agitated feelings for the beloved would never allow me to scrutinize him very minutely at short range. He seemed to me to be one of the kind of men we read about, lived but to die. If he ever got any enjoyment out of life, it must have been in making trouble for others. However, Miss Missionary thought he was about right; of course it is to be presumed that she knew him better than I did, but if such were her deep grounded conclusions of him, she had unquestionably known him in brighter days. His means had very probably been secured in any way possible, and possibly some unjust act of his past life was praying on his mind and kept him in this state.

The main attraction of the family, and the one who was the direct cause of my frequent visits in that direction, had a peculiarity which is quite common among certain classes, and that was, her great desire to perform some sort of missionary work. Some distant relative had been instrumental in founding a missionary school in Alaska, and this, together with the reading of literature along this line, had a tendency to incite such a

spirit within her.   It seemed strange to me how
she could love those little heathens in distant
lands with such an arduous love, and at the same
time detest the semi-clothed African descendants
in her own town.   Strange as it may appear, such
was the case, and every Christmas she would work
for weeks, preparing presents to ship to those
Alaskians.   In this, her intentions were unquestionably good, and she, perhaps, made many of
those little chaps happy at Christmas time.   Such
a spirit is, to a certain extent, a credit to anyone,
and if properly exercised, a commendable feature.

Mr. Spectacles succeeded in getting the Reverend
gentleman entirely under his control.   How he managed it, was never made known to me, but in the
very middle of the winter, when everything was
going on merrily as a marriage bell, he suddenly
broke forth with all his terror, and put his foot on
me for the final trip.   He who laughs last laughs
best, no doubt thought Mr. Spectacles, for he had
been decidedly on the shady side of life for some
months, but now, how that conversation we had
in the hammock some months before, did grind
on me and hum in my ears.   There was but one
thing now left to do, and that was, act the man
and die gracefully.   Friends thought it rather
strange that the heretofore warm friendship that
had existed, or presumably so, at least, between
me and the Missionary family, had come to so
·sudden a demise.   The old gentleman knew, and
I was not entirely ignorant of the cause.

The best of friends must part; so it was with the antique Reverend and myself. I have never crossed his path since, but I certainly thought at the time, if he did not increase the.fuel bill in the lower regions, when he took up his departure to dwell on the other shore, I would miss my guess.

Severing the bands of friendship between Miss Missionary and myself, were of a very different nature, and of such a character as not to warrant a reiteration here, but suffice it to say, it left such an impression in the archives of my memory's storehouse, that it will probably occupy until the bugle calls me hence. Had the earth opened and swallowed her up, it would have been but little difference to me, as circumstances were shortly such, that I was called from the place, and have never seen her since, and only indirectly heard from her once or twice. After being called away from the town, and thrown among strangers, the associations of the past would at times prey upon my mind in anything but a comfortable manner, and, regardless of what circumstances may be in such cases, there is always a sanguine feeling, though it may be in the face of the most unfortunate and darkest fate.

CHAPTER XVI.

NEW HOME AND NEW SURROUNDINGS—PARTING WITH FRIENDS BUT THE INEVITABLE FATE OF A STENOGRAPHER.

Parting with the many friends in Jolleyville was anything but an easy task. To think those scenes that had afforded me so many pleasant occasions, must be left in the back-ground, old faces to be forgotten and new friendships formed, presented to me anything but a pleasant thought. Being again tossed about on the billows of life's great ocean, among strangers, would not have been taken by me as a matter of choice. Such, however, is the inevitable fate of a stenographer; he must go where duty calls, and duty calls where the most bread can be earned by the sweat of the brow, and for me to do this, it called me a few hundred miles East, into a much larger place than Jolleyville.

Upon reaching the place that was to be my future habitation, some of the old feelings that had taken possession of me on former occasions, such as when I first planted my weary feet on the shores of Butchertown, took possession of me again, but having encountered some of the expe-

riences of life, I was much better prepared to en-
counter such difficulties, and I soon became reconciled to the rulings of merciless fate.

The winter just previously referred to, was '92–3,
and while circumstances were transpiring in rapid
succession, it crossed the mind of some intelligent
being in Jolleyville, to form a club for the purpose of endeavoring to learn something of what
was to be placed on exhibition at the World's
Fair, which was to open the following June. This
club was duly formed, and on the list of members my name appeared.

The meetings of this club proved not only very
interesting, but at the same time beneficial, and
many hot discussions often followed; especially
was this the case in regard to the Sunday opening
question.

On one occasion, with a view of ascertaining
how the various imaginations would differ, it was
voted that each member make a guess as to the
probable number in attendance at the Fair on the
first day of June, the one coming closest to the
number to receive a Columbian half dollar from
the club. The guesses were all securely sealed,
and a few weeks after leaving there, my surprise
may well be imagined, when receiving the much
coveted half dollar, together with a letter of con-
gratulations from the club.

Among the rules of the club was one to the
effect that all those visiting the fair, should, upon
their return, give before the club an account of

their trip, and incidents pertaining thereto, and in case any member should fail to return, he was to send a written report. As my lot was cast in other climes before attending the Fair, the following is a brief account of my visit:

"As I signed the iron-clad constitution of the Jolleyville Fair club last Spring, thus binding myself to give a free-handed account of my visit to the Fair, I, of course, went, under the impression that I would be called upon to make such a report upon my return; hence, to have a clear conscience, it will be necessary for me to give you a brief outline of my quiet and uneventful visit.

After planning for a couple of months for a visit to that much coveted spot, casting anchor on a number of dates on which I would start, and being disappointed an equal number of times, I finally placed the anchor on the fifteenth day of October and commenced to make arrangements and preparations to start on that date.

Like a country boy on the eve of a circus, I was quite restless on Saturday night, October 14th, but on Sunday morning I arose without being called more than once or twice, pushed myself into my store clothes, partook of a brief repast, and started for the depot. On arriving at the depot I found quite a number of people who all seemed to be "going some place" from the way they were crowding around. I said nothing to anybody for some time, but finally siding up to a fellow with a cap on, asked him what time the

train would start.   As trains were leaving in more
than one direction and on more than one road he
could not give me much satisfaction.   I then
stood still for a small period—of time, until a
large man with a hat on said, "This train for
Chicago." 'The idea at once flashed across my
mind that he was the fellow I had been looking
for, so I gathered myself up and scrambled into
the car, with the rest of the fellows, the fellows'
wives and their various and sundry children,
every fellow rustling for himself, and the conduct-.
or after us all.   (Before getting through with the
Fair I found this was but a foretaste, of what was
to follow.)

After the conductor had, as is usual on a train
leaving a large town where a number of trains
leave about the same time, pulled off about half a
dozen that were "on the wrong train" and
hollered "all aboard" once or twice, I and the
train started for Chicago.   We had not traveled
many miles when we shot into a long, deep, dark,
dismal tunnel, and when I thought of the terrible
mass of material, metal, stone, etc., above us, I
began to think about the time I had stolen the
peaches, and various other little mishaps and unjust acts of boyhood, and also a few of more
modern date.   The thought of how matters were
situated on "the other shore," pressed upon my
mind as it had seldom done before.   The smoke
was coming into the car so thick and fast the people

commenced to cough, but as every cloud has a silvery lining, so it was with this, and after a short time we again saw day,-

Soon after I got into the train at the depot, a young fellow that I have a slight acquaintance with, walked into the car and took the seat directly in front of me. He was a sort of an apology for a dude, but as green as a last summer's squash, and to say that his actions were amusing, is placing it mildly.

Nothing of importance took place, except eating, until we reached the town for which we had set sail, a trip of several hundred miles. It was in the evening when we reached the town and quite dark, neither of us having been there before and Mr. Squash very timid in a strange town. 'He, like me, knew his number, nothing more. After placing our feet on terra firma, we started up town, and while I insisted on waiting until we got up into town before making inquiry about our place of stopping, Mr. Squash could not wait, but marched up to a "Dago" candy stand and enquired for his number. The position assumed by Mr. Squash as he viewed the stuttering Dago over his glasses, can well be imagined. Of course no information was gained from him of any value, and after escorting Mr. S. one more block I courteously bid him goodnight.

Even though it was getting rather late in the evening, the street on which I was meandering was very crowded, and there were thousands of

fellows like myself—lost. I asked a man, with a
hat on, about where my number was, and he
pointed out the direction, and told me by going
several blocks in that direction I would find a
street car leading out toward the place I desired
to go.

My neglected appetite began to haunt me about
this time so I went into a place to get supper.
I dined, if such it might be called, came out
and walked, and walked and walked, and after
such action for about half an hour, much to
my surprise, came right ca-smack up to the depot
where I had unloaded myself. Discouraging
as this may appear it enabled me to get my
bearings again and I once more started for the
car line; got quite close to the place where I was
to take the car, but on crossing the street in front
of the Tribune building, there was so much con-
fusion, and the little boys with papers under their
arms, shouting about the phenomenal happenings
of the land, and, taking it altogether, I became
tangled up in the crowd, caught one of my little
feet on a slight elevation in the street, and ere I
could regain my equilibrium, the number of the
house I was looking for had evaporated from my
memory. I struggled around and got out on the
corner of the street, and I and the grip leaned up
against the building while we were trying to think
of that coveted number; finally, with the assistance of the umbrella, the wished for number tot-
tered across my mind, and we took the first car

suitable and reached the proper destination. In this connection, I might say there was a small vesuvius (eruption) on the back of my neck, which made things a little unpleasant at times; otherwise, I was having a fine (?) time in the town.

I slept a little, and after the sun arose, I started for the Fair, taking the boat from the city. Of course I was both pleased and surprised with the size of the Fair, but, feeling a little wrought up over my experience of the night before, together with the crowd at the gate and the pleasant feeling coming from the vesuvius on the back of my neck, I felt on the "scrapping" order, and considering it to be the most appropriate, I feasted my eyes upon the Krupp gun exhibit the first move. I then took a trip around on the elevated road, with a view of getting the lay of the land. After getting about two-thirds of the way around this, and being frightened by the immensity of the business and the crowd, I spied a sign, "United States Life Saving Station." I at once concluded I had better go over there and register before going any further.

"Shorty" had partially arranged to meet me at the Fair; we were to meet at the Administration Building telegraph office at noon, but, owing to a misunderstanding, I did not know on what date; so, at noon, I went over there, but no "Shorty."

There is no use telling you what I saw of the exhibits, as you have all viewed them. By four o'clock in the afternoon, I had walked until I was

completely "done up" and it seemed that further
locomotion on my part was completely out of the
question, but, being filled with blissful anticipation, I would agitate vesuvius a little, in order to
put new life into me, and again press forward.   I
will not tell the times I was "taken in" and swin-
dled out of my rapidly evaporating currency, but
this much I will say, I discovered before returning from the Fair, that I had guide books enough
to start a miniature library, none of which were
of any value to me or of any very great importance
to any one.

Tuesday passed about as did Monday, only on
that morning I went to the depot to meet "Shorty,"
and while there tangled up in such a crowd as you
never saw before, who should come surging by
but Julia G.   I was very much excited at the sight
of one I knew, and before I was aware of what I
was doing, gave vent to something like "Hello,
Julia!" and then she said something, and so did I,
and then all was over, the crowd passed on, and I
held my post.

Wednesday passed like unto the two days previous, only of course I was viewing different objects.   On this day I remained on the grounds to
see the fire-works, electrical fountain, etc.   I must
say I was very much disappointed with the electrical fountain, but the other displays of fire-works
were very nice.   Just before viewing the fire-
works, I had one of the most interesting experiences while there.   The trouble was, there were so

many of us remaining for the same purpose, and
we all wanted something to eat, and apparently
about the same time. , I kept looking for a place
that was not crowded, but soon became discouraged and went to a place where there was quite a
crowd, got my ticket and stood behind some people, waiting until they got through eating, when I
intended to fall into their place. I stood and
stood and stood, and the individual whom I was
waiting on, a very corpulent lady of the selfish
make-up, or, at least, I thought so, ate as I think she
never ate before, and still I stood. Other fellows
who came in after I did, had secured places, but
still I waited upon my large lady friend. I noticed
they were dishing up edibles at a terrible rate, but
never thought of the supply exhausting. However, after a certain length of time, my esteemed
lady friend completed her repast and took up her
departure. I immediately filled as much of the
vacuum left by her in the crowd as it was possible
for my slender form, (which was then more slender than ordinarily), and after waiting a short time
longer a waiter came along, and then, to my sorrow, I learned that they were just about out of
everything; there remained little, meagre pieces
of pie, ten cents per chunk, and some much wa-
tered milk, five or ten cents per drink, and I told
them I guessed not. I mosied out of the door,
sadder but wiser, although no more corpulent than
when I went in. The perfume from the departing
edibles had sharpened my appetite until all

thoughts of waiting until I went back to town, after the display of fire-works, for something to eat, was driven away and I sought other quarters. I next tried the Electricity Building, where they were cooking by electricity, or making a bluff at it, rather, as I learned afterwards. Here, I secured something in the line of eating, by paying desperately for it.

Thursday was the day of days with me, for I visited the Midway; Oh! such a mob, and such a time I had with my feet getting them through the crowd. Never in all my life did I see such bloodthirsty villians after ducats as those fellows out there were. I soon learned there was but one way to make anything like good progress while going into the swindling shows, etc., and that was to take out all the money you had, hold it out and let them take what they wanted and place the rest in your pocket.

I played with the Ferris Wheel for a short time, saw the donkeys in the streets of Cairo and would have taken a ride had I not been afraid, also saw the menagerie and many other exhibitions of money grabbing.

By Friday, I was becoming accustomed to walking around considerable and was taking in the Fair with a vengeance. Friday night I took in the city of Chicago by gas light, or a portion of it. About twelve o'clock I reached my place of stopping and placed my weary head to bed, however before doing so I balanced my cash, and at once saw that two or three more visits to Midway, and taking in a portion of the town again, would cause me to feel the effects of the stringency like unto as I had never felt it before.

Saturday morning I again started for the Fair. During the week I had captured a very severe cold, and like everything else at the Fair, it was BIG. Vesuvius had, however, somewhat subsided, and I was getting along fairly well. That day at noon on going to the telegraph office, I met the long looked for "Shorty." He was just the same little "Shorty," no larger, no smaller, and just as comical as ever. Among the places we visited that afternoon was your state building, and while in there we struck one of the most valuable things imaginable, a fellow selling needle threaders. Before I could stop "Shorty," he had purchased two, and much to my delight he presented me with one of them. We both rejoiced greatly, as there is no article of household and kitchen furniture of more value to us than such a piece of machinery as this. It will cause life to be materially lengthened for both of us, and the attachment of the useful little article known as a button to our paraphernalia will, in the future be looked upon as a pleasure instead of a curse. After visiting the Forty Beauties, and other scenes that had been omitted on the previous visit to the place, and scrambling over the fence to see Buffalo Bill's wild west show, and other things of equal worth, I started toward my stopping place,

turning my back upon the Fair for good. After
the usual trials, succeeded in getting my cranium
placed upon its downy couch about eleven fifty-
nine and three quarters p. m.

The next morning I started homeward with a
loaded brain but lean pocket-book. As I was going to the depot the thought suggested itself that
I purchase a morning paper from one of the
numerous little screeching individuals by the wayside; acting on the impulse of the moment the
contemplated purchase was accomplished, but
having my hands rather full I did not stop to un-
fold or read the paper until after reaching the depot. You may imagine the state of humor I was
then in when discovering the "kid" had sold me
a paper over a week old—I did not say anything,
but you will please pardon me for not penning my
thoughts.

In a short time the great Fair, together with the
busy city was left in the rear, and the beautiful
prairies of Illinois began to come to light on
either hand. When about one hundred miles out
we passed quite near the place of my extreme
childhood, and as I viewed the beautiful, broad
prairies that stretched before us, I thought well
might I say:

"Amid broad fields of wheat and corn,
The lovely home where I was born."

Passing along, I thought of the stories I had
heard my parents relate of the various experiences
of their childhood there, of the then undeveloped

plains, ox teams as a means of transportation, and
other things in comparison, and then to think of
the high state of civilization the country is now
in, we traveling at the rate of fifty miles an hour
with perfect ease, I wondered, was it within the
bounds of possibilities that the next generation
would witness such a change! Inventions have
gained ground more rapidly within the last fifty
years than they did for four hundred years before.
In 1492, the Indian of America used his pony and
canoe as a means of transportation; in 1792, four
hundred years later, they used small boats and ox
teams—how little progress in so great a period of
time! The railroad engine of 1860 is but a shadow
of the present day engine. Electricity has made
more wonderful development in the past ten years
than for centuries before; in fact, electricity has
reached that stage where we need not be surprised
at anything that may be accomplished by its wonderful power. When farming is so perfected that
all one will have to do is to sit in the house and
"press the button" to raise corn and potatoes,
milk the cows, etc., I think I shall again engage
in agricultural pursuits. The prospect is not flattering for this to be reached before Spring, anyway, and I will doubtless follow my present occupation for a short time yet.

After engaging in a few little difficulties which
are incident to traveling, I reached the place of
my habitation in fairly good condition. After
having become quieted down in my peaceful

abode, and all the outside world was wrapped in
slumber, I could hear such as the following pass
through my head: "World's fair guides, the only
official!" "Souvenirs, here! souvenirs here! souvenirs!" "Nice, fresh peanuts and popcorn, five cents
a—" "All the views of the ground, but five cents!"
"Shine, shine, mister, shine?" "Tribune, Globe
and any other leading papers! paper, mister, paper?" "Nice, ripe bananas, five cents a dozen, nice,
ripe!" "Shine, mister, shine?" "After the Fair,
After the Ball, The Cat Came Back, and all the
latest songs, only five cents, song, mis—" "This
way to the Fair grounds! this way, ladies and gentlemen!" "Don't make a mistake by thinking you
can see the Fair without a guide book, the only—"
"Chewing gum, five cents!" "Tribune, all about
the great railroad disaster!" "Shine, mister, shine,
only—." It was a repetition of what I heard at
the Fair.

Over a year having now passed since the dust
of Jolleyville was wiped from my feet, the old
landmarks have been crowded entirely to the
background, and new ones occupy the more con-
spicuous places in my memory and thought. New
acquaintances have been formed, and while the
old ones are not entirely forgotten, it is against
the laws of the wisely decreed nature that they
should be so fresh in mind as they were only a
year ago. What coming years may bring, time
alone will reveal. Perhaps the thought of friends
who once held sacred places in my storehouse of

memory will have been pushed entirely out, and but the appearance of their names or faces will recall old associations.

Among my new found friends, many of them are very congenial, some more than others, of course, some of whom will have a tendency to cause me to have a more pious feeling toward the old gentleman Missionary. Perhaps the following paper, which I read before a society of friends in my new place of abode, when called upon to write upon Whittier's "Among the Hills," will help them to better understand my position in regard to existing circumstances, and the tinge that even bitter disappointment may leave on one's life:

Scene, rural districts, country life in a hilly country. The writer portrays the place as immediately after a season of rain, everything fresh, green and inviting. He reaches the place in the evening as the shadows fall slowly, unceremoniously meets an idle milkmaid, and in the conversation which follows, the milkmaid relates: A fair maiden who had left the city for health, gains strength very rapidly, her health is regained, the ideal farmer meets her; apparently a case of love at first sight; after extremely brief preliminaries they are married; their cup of joy runneth over, as it were; he is elected to office, and peace and prosperity is their lot.

"Paint me as I am" is my motto, and never do I feel more impressed with it than when reading a poem like this. There is a peculiarity attached to every man's writings that enables those who are well read to distinguish the author by simply hearing the quotations. This proves to us that no one mind is capable of covering the entire scope of anything. The writings of some of our most noted authors, though their selections may be on altogether different subjects, the tenor of their articles have a striking familarity. We find one who gathers his thoughts from the homes, life and surroundings of the kings and queens; another writer, of perhaps the same popularity, seeks the quiet farm in the backwoods, for the ground work in his poem, while others will write such as will appeal to the sympathy of the reader, gathering his thoughts from the poor of the city. It is a strange but stubborn fact that almost invariably, whether the story be taken from the highest or lowest walks of humanity, whether it be taken from the royal family of the old world, or the humble fisherman of our land, there is intermingled with it an exchange of affections, as it were, that either winds up in matrimony or a disappointed life. Even W. T. Stead, who astonished the literary world in his "From the Old World to the New," in Review of Reviews, in Christmas ('92) number, had interwoven with it a love story that would have touched the tender portions of the heart of a criminal.

Whittier has made no exception to the rule in his "Among the Hills," hence it makes it rather a difficult subject for the wielder of a blunt pen to handle. In his description of the surroundings, he says:

"It was as if the summer's late
   Atoning for its sadness,
Had borrowed every season's charm
   To end its days in gladness.

I call to mind those banded vales
   Of shadow and of shining,
Through which, my hostess at my side,
   I drove in days declining.

We pause at last where home bound cows
   Brought down the pasture's treasure. * *

We heard the night hawks sullen plunge,
   The crow his tree mate calling,
The shadows, lengthening down the slopes,
   About our feet were falling.

And through them smote the level sun
   In broken lines of splendor,
Touched the gray rocks and made the green
   Of the shorn grass, more tender."

This certainly is the most pleasant time of the day in the country; the day's work is over, the shades falling, and the tired farmer, whether his deeds be evil or not, loveth the darkness, as that is his time of rest. If one has any feelings of love, it is more liable to sprout out this time of the day than any other, whether that love be for man or maiden, horse or cow, or the circumstances with which he is surrounded. To have all things work together in harmony and come out right, we must have the ideal milkmaiden. so here she comes:

"And weaving garlands for her dog,
  'Twixt chidings and caresses,
A human flower of childhood shook
  The sunshine from her tresses.

The sun-browned farmer in his frock,
  Shook hands and called to Mary;
Bare-armed, as Juno might, she came,
  White aproned from the dairy."

When we get to this part of the story, we grasp
the conclusion at once that the fairy maiden of
the butter laboratory is to be the heroine of the
drama, but we are disappointed; she but relates
the story of other days. She tells her tale, the
writer says:

"The early crickets sang; the stream
  Splashed through my friend's narration;
Her rustic patois of the hills,
  Lost in my free translation.

More wise, she said, than those who swarm
  Our hills in middle summer,
She came when June's first roses blow,   .
  To greet the early comer;

From school and ball and rout she came,
  The city's fair, pale daughter,   '
To drink the wine of mountain air,
    Beside the Bearcamp water.

Her steps grew firmer on the hills
  That watch our homesteads over;
On cheek and lip, from summer fields,
  She caught the bloom of clover.

For health comes sparkling in the streams
  From cool Chocura stealing;
. There's iron in our Northern winds,
  Our pines are trees of healing. * *

Beside her, from the summer heat,
  To share her grateful screening,
With forehead bared, the farmer stood,
  Upon his pitchfork leaning."

Here, the story drifts into that sort of intimate conversation that proves more affecting to be read to a more limited audience, and for that reason I make but a brief extract of what follows:

"She looked up, glowing with the health
  The country air had brought her,
And laughing said, you lack a wife,
  Your mother lacks a daughter.

He bent his black brows to a frown,
  He set his white teeth tightly,
'Tis well, he said, for one like you,
  To choose for me so lightly.

No mood is mine to seek a wife,
  Nor daughter for my mother;
Who loves you loses in that love,
  All power to love another."

I realize the fact that often, under the impulse of the moment, things are sometimes said that we do not exactly mean, and I think the individual who gives vent to such an expression as,

"Who loves you loses in that love,
  All power to love another."

must be under one of those impulses. We believe that love, like power, is a good thing if properly applied, but when it has the influence over one that it seems to have had over our hardy son of toil in this case, it can hardly be looked upon in any other than a spirit of disgust. If a person is really in this condition, he has my heartfelt sympathy. To abbreviate the narrative, we quote:

"And so the farmer found a wife,
  His mother found a daughter,
There is no happier home than hers,
  On pleasant Bearcamp water.

Flowers spring to blossom where she walks
  The careful ways of duty.
Our hard still lines of life with her
  Are flowing curves of beauty.

Our homes are cheerier for her sake,
  Our dooryards brighter blooming,
And all about the social air,
  Is sweeter for her coming."

This verse is one well worthy of example, that we might each live so those around us would feel our influence, and that we could help make life pleasant for others. We believe it is in the power of every individual to lead such a life as to make it pleasant or unpleasant for those around him. This being the case, it should be our ambition to live in that way that the world may be better for our having lived; that when we shall have been called upon to quit this earthly scene, the world will say, it is with sorrow we part with thee. It is not necessary to be egotistical to lead such a life as this, but let us treat every one as our equal, and that we may consider that day well spent when we have rolled a stone from our brother's pathway and placed a flower in its stead.

There is another verse, which we quote without comment, which reads:

"Her presence lends its warmth and health,
  To all who come before it;
If woman lost us Eden, such
  As she alone restore it."

As time passed on, it appears, or at least so the story goes, our farmer friend became ambitious and began to play the role of a politician; runs for office and is successful, and as he sails down life's pathway on flowery beds of ease, the proud possessor of both wife and office, we quote as follows:

"He has his own, free, bootless lore,
  The lessons nature taught him,
  The wisdom which the woods and hills,
  And toiling men have brought him."

Referring to the motto with which we started, viz: "Paint me as I am," I must say this poem pictures altogether in a one-sided manner. Were all lives on a wooded farm as this man's, we would all be out tilling the soil and watching for fair haired maidens from the city. True, we seldom find a writer who is perfectly honest in his descriptions; he always takes the best. This, as portrayed, is ideal farm life, he but shows up the sunshine; let us look on the other side of the fence, in the shade.

In this story, everything is working in perfect harmony, the earth seems to have put on her best robes, immediately after a heavy rain in the summer, harvest time, abundant harvest, the load of hay coming down the road, slowly, of course, the driver asleep, the ideal milkmaiden with the butter such as was never seen before or since, those exceptionally good cows putting in their appearance, just entering the gate, and then winds up:

"How rich
  And restful, even poverty and toil
  Become when beauty, harmony and love
  Sit at their humble hearth as angels sat."

But now for the other side of farm life among the hills, etc.: Two o'clock in the afternoon, sun so hot it almost melts one to the ground, no water to drink except some carried to the field in a jug, which has become so hot, sitting under the gympsum weed, that it almost hurts your throat. Picture, if you please, farm life as a reality under these conditions, a fellow plowing in the stumps, every few feet you strike a stump which jerks you and your horses crosswise, and at the same time have the cattle breaking through the fence at another portion of the field, destroying the corn, and in another place the hogs doing likewise, rooting up the potatoes. Ah,

"How dear to my heart are the scenes of my childhood,
When fond recollections present them to view."

After encountering such as this all day, retire to the house as the twilight gathers, and, after doing the necessary daily duties around the barn, there is anywhere from ten to twenty cows to milk. This is something that must be done three hundred and sixty-five nights out of the year, and this duty, after one has passed through what we have just outlined during the day, sometimes prove to be very arduous, especially if the cowlets are of the kind that kick. Those of us who are strangers to farm life will perhaps not appreciate this, but it is composed of those cold, stubborn facts that are made of as honest material as those outlined by

Whittier. Of course it is the other extreme, and in this, as in all other cases, there is the golden mean.

There are many pleasures the farmer enjoys we never realize here in the city, and there is no doubt but what thousands and thousands of our city poor would be ninety-nine per cent better off on the farm; in fact, I conscientiously believe the Lord intended our western plains should be more thickly inhabited than they are, and it seems almost cruel to keep children penned up in a little room in the city, when hundreds of thousands of acres of land lie in these United States yet undeveloped, where they might live as free as the birds of the air. But this, perhaps, plays no important part in our story.

It is a well known fact that the American is never satisfied until wrapped in the arms of death, and of course he never can be contented. If he lives in the country, he imagines the city is just the place for him; if he moves to the city, he sometimes has such a desire to get back to the old farm, he wishes he might have died in his youth, and so it goes. We are a restless, unsatisfied class of mortals at best, and we have long since reached the conclusion that anything like happiness can only be attained in this life by being contented with our lot, and in striving to fit and prepare ourselves for an inheritance in that land where contention and competition are strangers, and peace and happiness hold sway.

Stenographers, as a class, have every reason to be encouraged; stick together and work with a will.   The world is fast reaching the point where it cannot well afford to do without us. First of all, one in this business should strive earnestly to become proficient in his profession; stick close to business and do your best.

There is a great deal of excitement at times, caused by a new patent on the phonograph, and some enthusiastic agent gets hold of it, but we have the pleasure every time of seeing their boom fizzle out, and thus it always will be.   The trouble is, so many people have the idea inculcated into their cranium, that a stenographer is only a sort of a machine, and so he may be if he never tries to make anything else out of himself, but the live stenographer is ever up and doing something that will advance his employer's interests. How would it be with the phonograph? The minute the machinery is stopped, the key turned and the dictator· ceases to speak into the dormant tube, of what value is it? Perhaps he wishes an errand run, a letter copied, mailed, some one to fix up his private accounts, he will find his Mr. Phonograph sitting as quietly as he left it, while he runs his own errands and looks after his own accounts.   It might be argued his typewriter operator could do all this, and so he might, but if you are going to get some one that is competent to do anything, it would be just as well to hire a stenographer.

We have heard of prominent business men saying they could set the phonograph on their desk, talk into it at leisure and than send it in to be written off at the convenience of the type-writer operator. On routine work, where the one that did the typewriting was very familiar with the work and knew what was coming, it might be satisfactory, but on difficult matters it would make very poor sense, from the very fact that every letter would have to be written twice in order to enable any one not hearing it dictated, to properly punctuate it.

Even should they be introduced into general business, it would not hurt the lady stenographers much; it might give the boys a little rub, but we hardly think it probable that such a thing will be accomplished in this age. . Little experience with one of them will prove to most of us that they will have to be improved upon very materially before they will ever be much of a success in a business way. There will not be near the satisfaction to a business man to have to carry his machine over to his desk to talk to it as there would be in giving the military command of "Get your book," and see the poor steno scramble for life to get the words as they drop from his lips. There will not be near the satisfaction about discovering that he has said something wrong as there would be in cursing the stenographer, for if it had been taken in shorthand he could declare the stenographer was careless. Common reason will at once make

it apparent to business men, that it would be very
inconvenient to use such things, and I think there
is but little danger of their doing us any great
harm.   There may be a few cranks use them, but
they will be a class of people that a steno would
have a hard life with anyway, and then some of
us will have the satisfaction of trying to write
them off for them; they can't beat us on this point.

When any of you who hammer glass for your
bread become discouraged, think of others who
are performing like service, and renew your energy,
take courage and press forward with a will.   Perhaps, while you, in your leisure office hours, are
perusing the pages of this book, I will be strug-
gling with all my might, endeavoring to partially
read the mind of a rapid dictator who does not
talk loud enough to be heard, and then get a
swearing at, because "That's not the way I dictated it."   Such mournful sounds often creep
around my sanctum, and now comes that other
dreadful tone, "Take a letter," so I must leave
you.

THE END.

APPENDIX.

VALUABLE INSTRUCTIONS AND SUGGESTIONS FOR
STENOGRAPHERS, WRITTEN EXPRESSLY FOR
THIS WORK, BY MR. RUSSELL.

The successful man has many rivals, the unsuccessful none. The statement has been oft repeated that there are already too many stenographers, and to substantiate this, individuals have been pointed out who, having graduated from some school, have never been able to make a practical use of their knowledge.

There is but one road to success in any field of labor, and that lies through dense forests of impediments which must be removed by our own hands, until this pathway shall lead us out into the broad expanse where the constant tread of the successful ones has worn a thoroughfare.

It is a well known fact that the majority of those who graduate from short-hand schools come from the rural districts, with the intention of mastering the art, securing a situation and living in comparative ease in the city. After securing a diploma from school, the happy graduate wends his way to the business centers, confident that success has already perched upon his banner and that there is a vast vacancy in some business circle awaiting his arrival. But too often, although there may be a vacancy, there is a still larger one in the mind of the student, and the philosophy of nature teaches us that a vacancy can not be filled by a fruitless effort to draw from a vacuum. By this statement we do not wish to reflect upon the intelligence of the student, or to place below par the college diploma, but a few suggestions gained from practical experience may, we trust, prove of benefit to the beginner.

1st. The best equipped stenographer is not one who can exhibit a diploma and numerous letters of recommendation, but, if necessary, going without either of these, relies upon his work as evidence of his PRESENT worth.

2nd. "Mind your own business" is a proverb that should never be forgotten. The stenographer, unlike many other employees, is admitted at once to the secrets of the office; he becomes almost as conversant with the important matters of the firm as his employer himself, and to make these known outside of the circle in which they should be familiar, is to be guilty of betraying the interests which you are employed to serve.

3d. Too much stress cannot be laid upon gaining the unreserved confidence of your superiors. This can be accomplished only by giving absolute satisfaction, and this, in turn, is secured by studying their wishes and seeking to gratify them. Strict business methods must be observed, and when called upon to work over-time, as the stenographer frequently is, do so with a willingness that will forcibly demonstrate that you are laboring for the interests of your employer, and not merely to get your salary.

4th.   Do not swerve from the path of duty and indulge in extravagancies which the successful stenographers around you may enjoy, or, like the small boy who seeks to imitate his father by smoking a cigar, you may have cause to regret it. What we mean by this, is, don't think that you fill your position with such ability and dignity that the management will look over your personal faults, for there is no position, however well filled, but what may be occupied by others who are equally as able. In our experience we have known several proficient stenographers who, through carelessness, a disregard for office hours and other requirements, have lost the good will that their former faithful labors have merited.

In most places the stenographer is called upon to do a great deal of work other than letter writing, and to be in a general way acquainted with the details of the office will give to you a prestige not to be gained in any other way.   Promotion, generally, only comes through merit, and the stenographer who does only that which he is compelled to do around the office, manifests that his ambition rises no higher than the plane upon which he stands at present, and he may rest assured that the fond dreams of what to-morrow may bring

will never be realized, for the clouds of indo-
lence and indifference have bedecked the horri-
zon, precluding the rays which the sun of hope
has shed forth ere they have been able to accom-
plish their mission.

It is not the fond dreamer, but the incessant
toiler that subdues difficulties. When starting out
upon life's labors, we have had pointed out to us,
men and women of renown, who at one time occupied a very secluded position among the world's
busy throng, and as we have heard the story of
their success related we have felt like following in
their way as nearly as possible. But, alas! success is not to be attained in this manner. The opportunities which came to them have never been
presented to us, and we soon awaken to a realization of the fact that we are rowing in a different current entirely, and cannot successfully stem
the tide by our present movements. Observation
is one of the greatest factors entering into the
education of the practical man or woman. To
illustrate this point, we will relate an incident
which happened in our own experience, so far
back in our career that we have but a faint recol-
lection of its details.

On a bright spring morning, with several com-
panions, we started out early to spend the day
fishing. Arriving at the stream, one of the boys
immediately proceeded to prepare his line, and
had scarcely cast it into the water, when he expressed a shout of delight, as he pulled out a

large fish, weighing about four pounds. The rest of the boys ran to the same spot and all threw their line in the same place, evidently presuming that this was a favored spot where all you had to do was to pull out fish; but, to their dismay, they found the prize had already been taken, and that that special part of the stream was no more favored than any other. And still we were confident there were just "as good fish in the sea as have ever been caught." The idea we wish to convey in this, is to rely upon your own judgment, study your own surroundings, meet each emergency successfully, and when other laborers have good news to report, you will not be much less favored. No definite rule can be laid down, the pursuit of which will bring to us success; we must each master our own peculiar situation.

The great difficulty with most individuals who have failed in the past is, that they have not had the power of endurance to bravely face adversity and convert it into the channel of success. Napoleon once ordered his drummer boy to beat a retreat when he thought he had lost the day. The boy responded: "General, I don't know how to beat a retreat, but I can beat a charge that will strike terror to the hearts of the enemy." He did, and the very fact that he entered the army never having learned how to beat a retreat was so inspiring to the great Napoleon, that the boy's ambition was recognized and promotion was the natural result. Too many enter upon their labors in a half-hearted way, and they learn to "beat a retreat" before they have made a spirited charge. Many an individual has found the profession of stenography a stepping-stone to a higher plane, but, unlike some classes of work, the stenographer must be thorough and accurate, for he cannot write on the machine that which he has not been able to take in dictation. A large majority are satisfied with a speed of one hundred words per minute, simply because there are some positions they can fill at that speed, while the aim of all should be to write two hundred words per minute, for experience has proven that this can be done, and anyone who is satisfied with less, is lowering the standard.

The profession is now becoming much more crowded than it has been; competition has increased, and only the thoroughly competent stenographer is in demand at all. There are many things which contribute to success aside from those already mentioned, as it is evident that no stenographer can report a studied speech, delivered by an orator, unless he himself has become well read and in a general way acquainted himself with the subject under consideration. Life is short, however, and the field of knowledge so extensive that the reaper does not have opportunity to cover the vast territory even once, and the profession of stenography, like that of others, must soon be arranged to meet in a special way the requirements of each peculiar branch of business in which it is used. This will not only be of great advantage to the profession, but the business man as well, for the stenographer will then have no excuse for being ignorant of terms used in the special industry with which he has become connected. We do not expect at any very early date to see this system inaugurated, but the student who meets with any extraordinary success, has invariably done so by following a certain profession and becoming so thoroughly proficient in it that it has been difficult to replace his services. Many firms dislike to employ a new stenographer, because they are required to school them in their peculiar business for some six months before they are of much real worth. This should not be. The duties of the stenographer are so well defined in general, that there can be no excuse on his part for inefficiency.

The mistake is often indulged in, that because we have sufficient speed to meet present requirements we have therefore mastered the art, and many a student, after leaving business college, never thinks of continuing his studies for a year or two, until he has become so thorough that, if necessary, he could get up a text-book of his own. Garfield taught school at one time by keeping always just one lesson in advance of his class, and had he never informed us of this uncommon occurrence in his history, perhaps even those whom he taught would never have known it. Some of the best stenographers to-day are those who have by persistent study culled from some text book the necessary information and made a practical application of it. Their success has been due to the fact that when a situation was obtained, all the confidence they had was reposed in themselves, and never thought of such a thing as asking the teacher to solve the difficulties that arose. While we speak thus encouragingly to the beginner, and could, were we so disposed, point to numerous instances where success has been attained under the most adverse circumstances, this work would not be complete did it not contemplate, at least partially, the extensive field opening to the proficient, and the requisites necessary to meet future emergencies.

The anticipations of that which invention may bring about have entirely crushed the aspirations that have arisen within the minds of some, and they have seemingly left the field to be occupied by the phonograph and such other inventions as the ingenuity of the philosopher may bring forth. If the profession of stenography shall continue throughout the coming generations it will be due to the fact that the stenographer has proven himself to be more than a machine. The phonograph may record accurately every sound of the human voice and repeat it without having lost its individuality, but it is a machine and nothing more and can never be on a parity with the professional stenographer. We do not wish to be understood as saying that some of these inventions may not

in the near future take the place of some steno-
grapers, but wish to emphasize the fact that the
mind of man is more than a machine and must
always be so recognized. We are speaking now
to the professional stenographers, those competent to judge whether or not the position taken is
a tenable one. We are all familiar with the
many errors made in dictation by the ordinary
individual, in grammatical construction often and
quite frequent in choice of langauge. The phonograph MUST record every error and repeat it in
translation, and in this particular point is the
superiority of the stenographer shown. To
illustrate the point in view, we will give one instance where the stenographer acted as a machine
ONLY, without the exercise of that judgment which
must enter into all intelligent correspondence.

When we say that the stenogapher in question
was a lady, we presume none will infer from that
that we choose to use them as a mark of inferiori-
ty, for our purpose is far from this, our object
being only to adhere strictly to the truth. This
young lady, from some cause or other, was suffer-
ing from a spirit of drowsiness, and during dictation she quite frequently indulged in such con-
tortions of the facial features as to cause her employer to feel that he was perhaps somewhat un-
kind in talking to her until she had become so
weary. At length, quite overcome, she threw
her hands over her head and indulged in an audible "yawn" that told the story of her anguish.

Her employer ceased dictation, and, thinking that a little medical advice might be preferable to any other at' this time, said, ''For that tired feeling take some of Hood's Sarsaparilla,'' all of which the stenographer proceeded to write in her notes. You may well imagine his feelings, when reading over his correspondence and finding that he had given such advice to one of his customers, and had it not been for the circumstances surrounding the case, he doubtless would have insisted that he never gave vent to such an expression. This stenographer was perhaps accurate and thorough, but she was lacking in that judgment which should lend dignity to her position. The phonograph could have done all that she did, with the exception of exhibiting that tired feeling, but the stenographer should have done much more. By the recital of this occurrence we think we have proven the point at issue, that the stenographer is, or at least should be, more than a machine; but, if he is not, he can only be so considered.

Every rivulet has its source, but unless it shall gradually increase in volume it will soon become a stagnant pool, rather than a tributary which shall ultimately reach the ocean. The standard of our profession must be maintained to be the ocean of thought and understanding into which all our efforts flow, and, like the rivulets as they wend their way to the ocean, each has its peculiarities, and its waters may be distinguished from that of any other; but so soon as it reaches the great reservoir individuality is lost.   So we all form a component part of the stenographic world; some of us, as tributaries, may not be swelling to any large extent the dignity of our profession; if so, we are untrue to ourselves and guilty of retarding the progress of others.   If we are ever permitted to join the successful throng, it shall be because we have reached the harbor of success, and not because success has come to us.

We do not think that day will ever come when we shall be able to adopt a standard system of shorthand, for there are already too many divisions, the borders of which are all widening, to permit any such hopes to arise.   This, however, isa matter of secondary importance, as there is doubtless not a system extant to-day, but what, if properly mastered, together with such inventions as the student himself will adopt, will meet all the requirements of the profession.   The object to be sought is not so much a uniting of the various systems, so that we shall all think and write alike, as it is to become thorough in our own way of thinking.   If each shorthand student had a system of his own, he would be master of it, as no one else could be, and for this reason the student will never adhere strictly to the forms given by a text-book when there are opportunities afforded for improvement.   The ideas grasped by Pittman and others were not beyond improvemt, and, to adhere strictly to them in order that we may write a pure system, is to stunt the growth of our own individuality, and thus retard rather than encourage progressive thought.

The phonograph would never have been invented had the mind of Edison rested contented in the thought that present achievements could not be surpassed. All the agencies of nature will yet be called upon to exercise their powers, but even after all this has been accomplished we are satisfied that the decree of the Almighty shall not be changed, that "Man is Lord of his creations." Let the stenographer be as studious in his methods as the inventor possibly can be in his search for some undiscovered agency yet to be employed, and there will yet burst in upon us revelations more astonishing in their nature than the peculiar operations of those forces with which we are now unfamiliar. The age is a progressive one; the rays of light shed upon the mind of man in ages past have been preserved and handed down to us to-day, and with all this light streaming from behind us, the intelligence of to-day increasing the potency of its rays, the prospects of the future brighten, and we fancy we see emerging the coming man, who will be a type of the fullness of knowledge. Ours is but a minor branch which may contribute some light to the dawning day, and may it be so inviting and inspiring in its nature that, while the inventor lives upon the threshold of to-morrow, we shall not be found rocking ourselves to sleep in the shades of yesterday, wherein our ancestors passed away. We have no fault to find with the individual who dares to lift the curtain which surrounds futurity and prepare for coming events. If the fruits of his labors bring to him wealth, I know of none more worthy to be thus honored, and feel to admire that law which has been established, that, "The laborer is worthy of his hire," and "The idler shall not eat the bread of the laborer."

Let us not indulge in fond dreams of what the future stenographer may be, but let us always make the present superior to the past. We cannot afford to find fault with others because they have converted their log cabin into a palatial residence, for the same opportunities are afforded us. The momentum of a body will always tend to accelerate its present movements, and with an equal force applied, stimulating the effects of the past, we are satisfied that "THE STENOGRAPHER" will be looked upon as one of the important factors entering into the improvement of our commercial, educational and professional interests. When you have read "THE STENOGRAPHER" and become more thoroughly acquainted with his life and trials, let it be handed down to posterity with your benediction, forgetting the author whose experiences have been so much like yours.